THE WINEMAKER DETECTIVE

Twenty-two books
A hit television series

"The perfect mystery to read with a glass of vino in hand."

—*Shelf Awareness* starred review

"Wine lovers and mystery lovers alike will enjoy... Crime is a pretext for Epicurean moments in renowned landscapes.

—*Soleil Vert*

"A captivating blend of investigation and discovering wine country."

—*WinetourisminFrance.com*

"Will whet appetites of fans of both *Iron Chef* and *Murder, She Wrote*."

—*Booklist*

"An enjoyable, quick read with the potential for developing into a really unique series."

—*Rachel Coterill Book Reviews*

"Alaux and Balen are superbe writers... The series stays with you."

—*Netgalley Review*

D0813979

"The descriptions of the wine and the food are mouth-watering!"

"I love good mysteries. I love good wine. So imagine my joy at finding a great mystery about wine, and winemaking, and the whole culture of that fascinating world. I can see myself enjoying many a bottle of wine while enjoying the adventures of Benjamin Cooker in this terrific new series."

Mayhem in Margaux

A Winemaker Detective Mystery

Jean-Pierre Alaux
and
Noël Balen

Translated by Sally Pane

LE FRENCH BOOK 🔖

First published in France as
Sous la robe de Margaux
by Jean-Pierre Alaux and Noël Balen

World copyright ©Librairie Arthème Fayard, 2004

English translation copyright ©2015 Sally Pane

First published in English in 2015
By Le French Book, Inc., New York

www.lefrenchbook.com

Translator: Sally Pane
Translation editor: Amy Richard
Proofreader: Chris Gage
Cover designer: Jeroen ten Berge

ISBN:
Trade paperback: 9781939474384
E-book: 9781939474391
Hardback: 9781939474407

1

She was there, finally. Her laughter cascading down the stairs, the jar of blackberry jam left uncovered because she always forgot to put the lid back on, her quick hello as she dashed through the kitchen to start her morning run, and her clothes strewn helter-skelter in the middle of the bedroom. Cheerful, exuberant, curious, and messy. Finally, she was there for her summer visit, ready to stir Grangebelle out of its hot-weather lethargy.

Benjamin Cooker smiled as he looked at the picture on his desk. The colors were faded now, almost gone in some places. Margaux must have been six, maybe seven; she was wearing the little red coat with horn buttons that she ripped while climbing a fence. He remembered how she whimpered that day. To comfort her, he promised to ask the neighboring farmer to give her a ride on his tractor.

Benjamin's office was full of mementoes, most of which reminded him of his daughter. On his Empire-style table was a ceramic tile, painted in acrylic, from her kindergarten days. He still used it as a paperweight. Next to an eighteenth-century silver inkwell, a glass yogurt container covered with geometric designs on aluminum foil held all his pencils and pens. And on his Art Deco filing cabinet was her representation of a windmill: sunflower seeds, dried beans, and lentils glued on cardboard. Over time, Margaux's Father's Day gifts had become more sophisticated. She had dipped into her piggybank toward the end of junior high school and given him a brochure published in the nineteen thirties by the Margaux Winemakers Union. "The best wine in the world," it read.

A true elixir for a long life! Margaux wine revives the body without dulling the mind. Your breath stays clean and your mouth cool, because it's strong but not overwhelming. Its color is gorgeous and its bouquet incomparable. Its supremely delicate taste gives it unparalleled distinction. When you buy MARGAUX, you buy HAPPINESS and HEALTH.

When his mind wandered during the long hours at his desk, Benjamin liked to reread the brochure, which he had framed in bronze-colored wood. It took him back to a carefree time of innocent enthusiasm and strong convictions.

The winemaker remembered himself as a youngster with corduroy shorts and scraped knees, a well-bred and lonely boy who, long before creating the acclaimed *Cooker Guide* series sold in bookstores all over the continent, had awakened his senses in the wine cellar of Grangebelle, the family estate in Médoc where he now lived with his wife, Elisabeth. His grandfather, Eugene Frontenac, although not the best winemaker in the area, had garnered considerable respect when it came to tasting wine from the barrel and giving his opinion. The old man had a way with words and always found the right one, the precise comparison, the judicious observation to describe so many subtle aromas—fig, roasted almond, violet, candied prune, caramel, musk, brioche, gunflint, hay, cacao, flint, licorice, Murelle cherry, candied fruit, or fern. Benjamin had been his eager student, and well before he even put a glass of wine to his lips, he had learned a world of descriptive variations, which no doubt helped him rise in the ranks of notable wine tasters.

Indeed, no one questioned Benjamin Cooker's expertise in the complex area of wine tasting. It was the very core of his business. The nearly thirty organic acids found in wine, its twenty-some varieties of alcohol, and more than eighty esters and aldehydes made for a heady mix he would sniff, swirl, and describe. Despite the sometimes dramatic performance of chewing and slurping,

Benjamin knew that he didn't detect a wine's flavor on his tongue, but instead in his nose. It was his keen olfactory sense that allowed him to distinguish the four hundred or so aromatic compounds at work. That was as far as the science went. The rest involved sensory memory and art—although he knew that some skeptics called it bull. Benjamin sometimes returned to his moments with his grandfather on the rare occasions that he felt at a loss for words.

"Benjamin, come join us for tea," Elisabeth called from the kitchen. "We'll have it on the terrace." Her tone was that particular variant of nonchalant that meant she didn't want him to dawdle.

He grumbled and left the relative coolness of his office to join his wife and daughter. The July air was oppressive, dry, and heavy, without the slightest promise of a storm. He sat down in his chair and sank his spoon into the jar of jam. But before he could put it to his lips, a drop of the gooey sweet plopped on his shirt.

"Benjamin, you're such a child," Elisabeth said as she poured his Darjeeling. "At least you didn't use your finger."

He winked at Margaux, who bit her lip to suppress a smile. They had long ago established a complicity. It was based on childish games, silly gestures, and harmless pranks, along with an occasional long discussion about the tides, the injustice of God, food cooked in goose fat, the works of Chateaubriand, the art of polishing shoes, and the architecture of the Cordouan lighthouse. Benjamin had never been an authoritarian parent. He had left Margaux's basic upbringing to his wife. To be sure, there was some tension between mother and daughter during the teenage years, but the two of them had managed to find a balance, especially after Margaux moved to the city to study business.

Elisabeth had adapted well to her daughter's decision to study in Bordeaux and enjoyed visiting her. It was an opportunity to get away from the Médoc, do some shopping, have uninterrupted time with her daughter, and discuss large and small matters, which ranged from politics and social issues to food and fashion.

"I saw you ladies gawking over an issue of *Femme Actuelle*. If you're planning to hit the shops later, please remember that I don't have a surgeon's income."

"It was *Marie Claire*, Papa, and you should have seen that pair of designer jeans," Margaux said, winking at her mom.

"I'm sure you'd look quite fetching in them with a pair of embellished heels," Benjamin said, sipping his tea.

"Give it up, Papa. You're useless when it comes to fashion."

"I wouldn't say useless. I just have traditional tastes."

"You say traditional," Margaux said, pouring herself another cup of tea. "I say fuddy-duddy."

"Now you've gone too far, young lady," Benjamin shot back, grinning. "And I'll have you know that I do splurge on clothes from time to time."

"Yes, to replace that same Loden coat, herringbone shirt, tweed jacket, or English shoes that you've worn since before I was born."

"Touché, my darling fashion queen."

"These are delicious, Papa," Margaux said, changing the subject and grabbing another almond meringue cookie.

"Authentic *macarons de Saint-Émilion*. There's more to that town than wine. The recipe dates back to 1620."

Benjamin finished his tea, set down his china cup, and glanced at the clock. "We have to get going, girls."

"Don't worry, Papa. I don't need long to change."

"We'll be down in just a minute," Elisabeth chimed in.

Considerate. Yet another of his beautiful wife's characteristics. Without breaking a sweat, she could turn out a dinner rivaling any served up in a two-star restaurant. Then she could sit down with her guests and discuss world affairs. And she hardly ever complained about his work, which required him to be away from home much of the time. He felt truly blessed to have her at his side.

The winemaker stood up and gave his wife and daughter an affectionate look before heading back to his office, if only for the few minutes Elisabeth and Margaux needed to get ready. An article for an Australian magazine that he had spent two days laboring over still wasn't finished.

He would have preferred putting off his work. Grangebelle's stone construction had kept the house relatively cool during the past month. But a person had to be either a martyr or a fool to do anything in heat that was this stifling. The weather forecasters weren't seeing any signs of a letup, either. Some were even predicting a heat wave worse than the one the region had experienced in 2003. The vineyards were beginning to show troubling signs, and now there was the threat of a drought.

Benjamin trudged back to his desk and made some easy revisions, crossing out a few redundancies and reworking a paragraph here and there. Then he decided he had done enough. Upstairs, he could hear Margaux going from room to room in her heels.

"Did you get into my makeup again?" Elisabeth called to her daughter, sounding more curious than irritated.

"We're taking off in fifteen minutes!" Benjamin yelled up the stairs. He stepped into his own bathroom at the end of the hall, having been crowded out of the one upstairs many years earlier.

He showered quickly, shaved, and splashed on some *Eau d'Orange*, which he preferred on hot days. It was much lighter than his usual *Bel Ami*. After he put on his sky-blue shirt, he took a good look at himself in the mirror. He was rare that he lingered before his reflection, and whenever he indulged in this dangerous exercise, he was invariably surprised to see how he had aged. Eyelids not quite as high, a bundle of wrinkles at the corners of his eyes, and a heavier chin. At this stage in his life, Benjamin, the product of a London father and a Bordeaux mother, disparaged his visage: a mix of arrogance and innocence, a bit aloof and yet jolly.

Elisabeth and Margaux were waiting for him when he emerged from the bathroom.

"You look fabulous, ladies! Really superb."

"And you thought you'd be waiting for us. We've been cooling our heels while you've been splashing on your *Eau d'Orange* and staring at your handsome face in the mirror," Elisabeth said, playfully pinching his cheek.

"Do these pearls make me look like an old lady?" Margaux asked, running her fingers over a three-strand choker.

"Not at all." Benjamin said. "Pearls never go out of style. They're timeless."

"As if you'd know about style, Papa. I think they look kind of matronly."

"Your father is right. That choker looks very nice on you. Trust him for a change."

"When I say 'matronly,' I mean like some fussy old rich lady. You know the type."

"Oh, I do," Benjamin chuckled. "But you have nothing to worry about. You have inherited your mother's natural class."

Elisabeth brushed his cheek with a kiss.

"Simplicity is the ultimate sophistication. Your father loved that da Vinci quote, didn't he, Benjamin?"

Like Benjamin himself, Paul William Cooker had a talent for reeling off quotes, as well as coming up with his own expressions. A London antique dealer, he collected sayings with the same passion that he acquired boxes, tables, and chairs: in profusion. They filled his mind, just as his old things filled the store. Some of his expressions had absolutely no truth and were even a bit foolish, but they circulated in the family as if they were the indisputable truth.

"Benjamin, you're looking quite handsome at the moment," Elisabeth said, giving her husband a head-to-toe look-over. "Casual but stylish. You're just my type."

"I envy the two of you," Margaux said. "How do you manage to still love each other after thirty years of living together?"

"Well, I'm very easy to live with," Benjamin said, giving his wife a wink. "There's no other explanation."

"No comment," Elisabeth answered, returning her husband's smile.

They walked outside, where Benjamin's 280 SL convertible was waiting for them. He turned on the ignition, and Elizabeth and Margaux climbed in beside him. He was glad that they hadn't asked him to put the top up to avoid getting their hair mussed. It was a pleasure to be driving with the sun setting at their backs and a warm breeze softly brushing their faces and caressing their necks.

Benjamin drove at a moderate speed to enjoy the moment and let Margaux take in the landscape of her childhood. His daughter had been living in New York for three years, and even though she was sometimes homesick, she didn't regret her decision. Her position as manager of a company that imported gourmet foods from southwestern France had been an opportunity seized at just the right time. The salary was more than decent. Her two-room Greenwich Village apartment was charmingly furnished, and she had acquired close friends who made her feel at home in a huge city where every moment was lived with intensity.

They passed through the villages of Cussac-Fort-Médoc, Arcins, and Soussans and turned left toward Château Margaux. Benjamin slowed down as he passed the sign and kissed Elisabeth's neck. Margaux! How many bottles had borne her name! A name that for centuries had resonated throughout Bordeaux and beyond like the promise of ecstasy.

The building loomed at the end of a road lined with tall plane trees. Its sumptuous Palladian façade was a Greek temple lost in a sea of emerald vines. It had been built at the beginning of the nineteenth century by the same architect who had designed the Bordeaux opera house. Benjamin parked the convertible beside dozens of other cars and gave Elisabeth and Margaux a few minutes to brush their hair. They got out and followed the lamps that lit their way to the gardens flanking the east wing. With glasses in hand, guests were chatting happily. Beyond the tables covered in ecru linen, gold-rimmed dishes, and candelabras, a quartet was playing Baroque music at a volume that complemented the atmosphere, a sure sign that the musicians were experienced and highly skilled in the art of providing background music. Every member of Bordeaux's elite winemaking society was here on this night.

Benjamin could see Elisabeth and Margaux relax as they took in the sea of guests and realized that they had dressed appropriately for the occasion. The hosts had wanted this dinner affair to be lovely but also comfortable. Few men were wearing ties, and the women were in light-colored linen suits and summer dresses with modest necklines.

Benjamin was immediately surrounded by property owners who politely asked how he was doing but mostly wanted his advice. Elisabeth greeted some of the wine merchants' wives she had met at dinner parties and soon found Hubert de Boüard and his wife, who were close friends and the owners of a premier grand cru estate. After managing to escape a paunchy banker who was worried about his heavy investment in grand crus, Benjamin beat a path to his wife, who was taking a glass of Champagne from a server.

"Are you bored, my sweet?"

"Not in the least. Did you know that the Boüards are leaving for Cap Ferret two days from now, just like us? We'll have to have dinner together."

"I'll leave all the planning in your capable hands," Benjamin replied as he waved to a couple whose names he couldn't remember.

"Who is that handsome young man hanging around Margaux?" Elisabeth asked, nodding in the direction of the orchestra.

Benjamin looked over and tensed. A man who appeared to be in his thirties was casually sitting on a table and whispering in his daughter's ear.

Margaux let out a laugh, revealing her perfect-ly white teeth. For the first time, Benjamin was witnessing his daughter in a game of seduction he could never have imagined.

"I think it's Antoine Rinetti," he murmured, his jaw tight. "The new manager of Gayraud-Valrose."

"He's rather young to be in charge of such a château," Elisabeth said. Benjamin picked up a hint of admiration in her voice.

"A Swiss insurance company bought the estate. They brought him in to get the finances in order."

"He's not from here?"

"From Nice. Can't you tell? Flashy suit, a tie that looks like it cost close to a thousand euros."

"You sound jealous, Benjamin. But your daughter is a young woman now. And I think she has pretty good taste."

Benjamin looked at Elisabeth and tried to smile. "Stop teasing," he said.

Although he had accepted Margaux's transition to adolescence and knew, at least intellectually, that she was now a young woman, she was still his little girl. To him, Margaux would always be the child with bright eyes, rosy cheeks, and pixie nose hugging her teddy bear and whimpering over the slightest boo-boo. The insistent gaze of this young man in an Italian suit seemed indecent and would have even been repulsive, were he not so handsome.

2

The following day was grueling. Awake at the crack of dawn, Benjamin Cooker put on his country uniform: beige cotton pants, brown checked shirt, khaki vest, and Timberland shoes. He poured food into Bacchus's dish and apologized to the Irish setter for not taking him out for a walk. Then he quickly drank two glasses of mineral water and took off for his office on the Allées de Tourny in Bordeaux to check his mail. He left written instructions for Jacqueline, his secretary, who would not be in until around eight-thirty. A lab report written by his colleague Alexandrine de la Palussière was lying on a shelf. He scanned the document and decided that he knew enough about the parasitic maladies plaguing some estates around Blaye. The bronze clock showed seven forty. He phoned his assistant.

"Be ready, Virgile. I'll be at your place in five minutes."

He hung up, gulped a cup of cold tea, and went down to the street to get his convertible to drive to Virgile's place. When he reached the corner of Rue Saint-Rémi, he found his assistant leaning against the building, looking totally relaxed. He was wearing a white T-shirt, weathered jeans, and navy-blue sneakers. Virgile grinned when he spotted Benjamin and slid into the passenger seat.

"Morning, boss. It's going to be hot as hell today. They're predicting ninety-five degrees in the shade."

"Unfortunately, my boy, you won't be spending much time in the shade. Everyone's worried about the effects of the weather on the grapes. We're visiting all our clients on the right bank, toward Camblanes-et-Meynac, beginning with Château Brethous."

"That's fine with me! Cécile and Thierry make a strong cup of coffee, and I really need one."

"Just don't tell me what you did last night. I'll have no sympathy."

Under a leaden sun that burned the skin and dried the lips, they spent the entire day checking the health of the vines. They conscientiously visited a dozen properties, surveying the land without stopping to rest. Many of the vines had been pruned at the usual time to intensify the aromatic and tannic concentration of the grapes. But considering how hot and arid the summer had become, this traditional thinning had proved to be much too early. Who could have known? If the weather didn't break soon, the vintage would suffer, and the region's growers were anxiously watching the sky in hopes of spotting even a few lifesaving clouds. The estate owners couldn't even predict when the grapes would be ready to harvest.

Benjamin and Virgile were thirsty and exhausted at the end of the afternoon. They returned to Bordeaux and ordered two large lemonades on the terrace of the Régent.

"I'm afraid I'll fall asleep in the shower," Virgile said, sighing and sipping his beverage.

"We'll be doing the same thing tomorrow in Léognan, Virgile. We need to focus on the soil conditions and the quality of the grapes. If we have any hope of controlling the winemaking process, it's absolutely imperative that we get a grasp of what's happening to the grapes."

"So no vacation then?" Virgile ventured. Was that a whiny note in Virgile's voice?

"For now, just worry about not falling asleep in the shower, Virgile! We'll talk about your vacation later. But I wouldn't get my hopes up. At this point, it doesn't look likely."

Benjamin didn't bother to add that even though Elisabeth and Margaux would be at Cap Ferret, he wouldn't be spending the usual amount of time with them. There was just too much work to do.

Instead of returning to his office, Benjamin left for Grangebelle after finishing his lemonade, paying his bill, and dropping off Virgile at his apartment. As soon as Benjamin drove past the stone pillars and turned onto the driveway lined with Japanese cherry trees, Bacchus got up from the grass to welcome him. But it wasn't his usual energetic greeting. The setter's Irish origins were not an advantage in this infernal heat. The dog's tongue was hanging out, and his gait was sluggish. Even his bark was feeble. Distracted by the dog's lethargy, Benjamin almost slammed into a red Porsche 911 turbo parked in the courtyard.

Margaux was on the doorstep, hugging her mother good-bye. Antoine Rinetti was watching. He was wearing a sporty getup and a whimsical tie that he had probably purchased in some luxury boutique on the Côte d'Azur.

"Don't stay out too late, dear," Elisabeth said. "Remember, we're leaving for Cap Ferret in the early afternoon, and I'm counting on you to help me finish packing."

"Let me sleep at least until ten, Maman."

Benjamin ran a hand over his face and suppressed a grimace. He got out of his Mercedes convertible. Its antique chrome and burr elm dashboard seemed like relics, compared with Rinetti's flashy sports car. The young Gayraud-Valrose manager greeted him with the obsequious confidence of a brat with a string of diplomas and opinions. Margaux ran to meet her father and kissed him on the cheek.

"Antoine asked me out to dinner, so you two lovebirds will have the house all to yourselves tonight," she said with her characteristic warmth, which he had never been able to resist.

"Well, have a nice evening, sweetheart," Benjamin found himself replying. He deliberately avoided eye contact with the young man from Nice.

His daughter and her date got in the Porsche. It took off, sending a volley of gravel toward the Anduze vases lining the house and outbuildings. Feeling dejected, Benjamin turned to his wife.

"What could Margaux possibly see in a man who drives a car that ostentatious?"

"It's not very understated, I'll admit."

"I just hope his driving is better than his taste in cars and ties."

"Let's hope that heaven hears your prayers."

"I've always thought that expression was a bit silly," Benjamin grumbled. "I'd rather have heaven listen to me."

The evening was gloomy and tense. For dinner, they just nibbled cheese and tomatoes drizzled with olive oil. Elisabeth tried her best to get a conversation going, but Benjamin was in a foul mood. Exhausted from the day's work but too wound up to relax, he soon disappeared into his office to arrange his files. He worked methodically, completely absorbed in a task that he could complete without actually thinking.

He slipped into the bed at midnight, gave his sleeping wife a cursory peck on the neck, and brooded until he fell asleep. Three hours later, the telephone jerked both Elisabeth and him awake. And in a voice that unbelievably had a hint of cheerfulness, the police officer told them that Antoine Rinetti's Porsche had been found on fire not far from the Quai de Paludate.

3

There was something depressing about the harsh light. It was barely seven in the morning, and the city was getting ready to face another day under the oppressive sun. Elisabeth and Benjamin looked out the expansive window, covered with fingerprints that attested to the nervous waiting of families that had been here before them. A nurse had come to tell them that the operation was almost over. The doctor would be out soon to give them the results.

They held hands. Benjamin turned his gaze from the sky just above the rooftops to his wife. She was pale and shaking. Elisabeth had been in tears all the way to the hospital, and Benjamin feared he would have to stop the car to let her vomit. She was still feeling nauseated. Benjamin pulled his wife closer, but there were no words that would help. He didn't even think she could hear them.

They waited for more than an hour, oblivious to everything around them: the others waiting for news of their loved ones, the nurses passing through, the ringing of cell phones. They responded only when the surgeon appeared, still in his scrubs. He needed a shave, and he looked tired. But he was smiling.

"Your daughter is a fighter," he said.

"Thank God!" Elisabeth let out. She released Benjamin's hand to dab her eyes and mouth with a tissue.

"The operation was a complete success. We repaired the tibia and fibula fractures in her left leg. She'll have some screws and bolts, but that's a small price to pay. I must warn you, though: the recovery might be long, and she'll be wearing a cast."

"How long?" asked Benjamin, finally able to breathe normally.

"A month, maybe longer. I want to be cautious. Your daughter also suffered a mild cranial trauma, and we need to keep an eye on that. It doesn't appear to be anything serious. No skull fracture, just what appears to be a mild concussion. She may have some headaches in the next few days, but she should be fine. At any rate, she's a very lucky young woman. The outcome of that accident could have been far worse."

Benjamin gave the doctor a faint smile. Margaux had always had a stubborn streak. Now it had served her well. She had been bullheaded enough to refuse to die.

"She was ejected at the moment of impact," the doctor continued. "Her head struck the top of the windshield, so her face wasn't lacerated by any of the glass. She would have needed a plastic surgeon if she had struck the windshield a few inches lower. As I said, she's a lucky young woman."

"And the driver?" Benjamin asked, biting his lip.

"The prognosis is less optimistic for her companion. He was transferred to a burn unit, where he was put in an induced coma. It's the only way to make the treatment tolerable."

"So it's serious," Elisabeth said.

"Yes, I'm afraid so. He managed to extricate himself from the fire, but his clothes were in flames. At the very least, he'll be disabled and disfigured after years of skin grafts, provided they aren't rejected. But we aren't there yet. We'll have a better idea of how he's doing in a few days."

"What a shame," Elizabeth sighed. "Can we see our daughter?"

"She's in recovery right now. You can see her as soon as we take her to her room. That should be in about two hours."

They thanked the doctor. Benjamin, usually reserved with people he hardly knew, gave the man's arm a warm squeeze before shaking his hand.

The doctor seemed embarrassed and said he had merely been doing his job.

They decided that Elisabeth would stay at the hospital and wait for Margaux to get out of recovery. Benjamin needed to stop at his office to take care of some pressing matters. He would come back as soon as possible.

A wave of heat struck him as soon as he stepped outside. Wiping his forehead, which was already wet with sweat, he scanned the street for shade. Choosing the side lined with a few stunted trees, he checked his cell phone for messages while walking toward his car.

He immediately recognized Virgile's worried voice.

"I just spoke to Jacqueline. She told me what happened. I can't believe it. Whatever you need, I'm here for you, boss. Just let me know. I'm thinking of you. And please give Mrs. Cooker a big hug for me."

There was a second message. This caller's tone had more authority. It was almost demanding.

"Hello, Mr. Cooker. Inspector Barbaroux here. I heard about your daughter. Call me at the office. I have some information for you." Benjamin had helped the police inspector on some investigations in the past, so his call was not much of a surprise.

Benjamin's first call was to Virgile, who, since early morning, had been walking the terroir of Léognan by himself. After reassuring him about Margaux, Benjamin asked for a brief report on the state of the vines. The assistant had found a trace of parching, but the symptoms weren't alarming. Virgile advised following up with another evaluation in a week.

The conversation with Barbaroux was concluded much more quickly—just the few seconds it took to write down the address of a police depot in the industrial zone of Mérignac. Benjamin could not get any explanation from the man.

He took the road leading to the airport and turned toward a site that seemed to correspond with Barbaroux's directions: concrete and sheet-metal structures rising from cracked asphalt. Ghostly streetlamps, billboards, and roundabouts provided the only visual relief. Benjamin crawled along aimlessly, turning left and right, his nose glued to the windshield as he searched for the depot. After asking for directions a good ten times, he finally found the building. Barbaroux was waiting for him outside, his forehead dripping and his face beet-red. His unwashed shirt was stained yellow in the armpits. Barbaroux nodded when the winemaker came up to him with his hand extended.

"No hand-shaking in this heat," the inspector said, wiping his hands on his pants.

They entered the building, where technicians in blue smocks were working around and under vehicles perched on platforms. Barbaroux went directly to the charred body of the Porsche 911 turbo. Not much remained of it. The car was barely a blackened heap of scrap with a bitter odor that stung the eyes and nose.

"I guess your daughter will come out fairly well," Barbaroux said without turning to look at Benjamin.

"You guess right, in fact," Benjamin replied, surprised by the inspector's choice of words.

"According to the report from the rapid intervention team and the preliminary findings provided by the Emergency Medical Assistance Service, I suspected that she would pull through. You have reason to be thankful."

Barbaroux had the blunt and standoffish bearing of shy people who were in the habit of hiding their feelings under thick armor. He talked tough to avoid showing any signs of emotion. Benjamin wasn't fooled and listened without paying attention to the inspector's old-fashioned display of masculinity.

"As soon as I found out that it was your daughter, I had the car transferred to the depot to have it assessed."

"Why would you do that, Inspector?"

"We want to determine the cause of the accident, Mr. Cooker."

"Do you suspect foul play?"

"You never know with a man of your stature."

Benjamin's legs felt weak, and he suspected it had little to do with the heat. Could someone have targeted his daughter? He took a deep breath and tried to maintain his proverbial calm.

"Our guys got on it right away, and they gave the results directly to me. No one else has read the report, and I wanted to talk to you before sending it through official channels. Consider it a token of my friendship."

"And what does it say?" Benjamin asked.

"Some very interesting things. The car crashed in a roundabout at the end of Quai de Paludate. It hit a tree. This guy Rinetti was driving like an idiot. He had to be going more than eighty miles an hour in the middle of the city—you get the picture. He lost control negotiating the turn, and he braked too late. The tire marks on the asphalt leave no room for doubt. The impact was extremely violent. I won't go into detail. Your daughter wasn't wearing a seat belt, and ironically that's what saved her."

Benjamin did his best to avoid shaking. His daughter had been in that car with the loony tune! He said nothing and followed Barbaroux's movements as he stooped under the torched frame.

"When the car hit the tree at full speed, it didn't take long to catch fire," the inspector continued. "In the Porsche 911, the gas tank is in the front. You see? Right here. And since it was night, the headlights were on. One spark was all that it needed."

J.-P. ALAUX & N. BALEN

The winemaker suppressed another shudder and turned to get a closer look at the point of impact.

"If you scoot over a bit more, you'll see what the investigators found. Don't be afraid of getting dirty. It's worth a look. Come over here and you'll see better. Right there: the brake-fluid hose is sliced precisely in this spot, near the disk."

"You mean to say someone cut it?"

"Our techs are sure of it. The hose has three layers: the tube, a metal layer, and a rubber layer. Only shears make a cut that clean. There's no doubt. This was a malicious act."

"Was the hose on the other side also severed?"

"No, the system is intact on the left side. No need to slice both to cause an accident. All you need to do is wait a little longer for the fluid to drain out. The person who did this gave the driver enough time to get from Saint-Julien to Bordeaux, eat at a restaurant, go to a nightclub, have a last drink, hit the brakes two or three times just to show off, and crash in the next curve."

"Are you sure?"

"As if I had been there myself, Mr. Cooker."

The two men were quiet for a while as they gazed at the wreck.

"Mr. Cooker, do you know anyone who would want to harm your daughter?"

Benjamin looked up and stared at the police officer. He was speechless.

"Do you have any enemies? Anybody who may have tried to get at you by hurting your daughter?"

Benjamin finally spoke up. "Inspector, I'm a civilized man working in a civilized business. I may ruffle some feathers with my tasting notes, but I'm always fair, and I have dedicated my life to helping winemakers make a better product. It's out of the question that I could be the target here."

"Your ratings can make or break a château, Mr. Cooker. You understand that my question is legitimate."

"Furthermore, my daughter didn't even know Mr. Rinetti before yesterday. Their date was spontaneous. There couldn't have been time to plan... What would you call it, a hit?"

The two men walked around the car. Benjamin sniffed it with a mix of repulsion and shock. His daughter had just experienced a brush with death. And according to the police inspector, it wasn't a random accident.

"What a waste," Barbaroux sneered. "When you think of all the dough one of these things costs. Close to two hundred grand, I figure."

"The equivalent of some nice acreage in the Premières Côtes de Bordeaux," Benjamin said tersely.

"Ah, yes. You have to have money to blow to buy a baby like this. Too bad it all went up in smoke."

"I imagine that some people who can afford a toy like this would think nothing of buying twenty-five acres of Pomerol or Saint-Émilion."

"Yep. In my line of work, I occasionally come across folks who don't know what to do with their money. Things that you and I dream of acquiring, they buy as nonchalantly as toothpaste at the drugstore. But I can't help wondering how these people earned their cash. I've investigated a few, and what I've found has been enlightening, believe me."

"I'm sure it has."

"You couldn't begin to comprehend the ways that people get rich and what they're willing to do to become wealthy. I tell you, it's disgusting."

"Could you get me some information on Rinetti?"

"Why, Mr. Cooker? The sabotage is a police matter. We'll be handling the investigation."

"Fair enough, but I'd appreciate it if you'd pass along whatever you find on him."

"Would you, by any chance, be thinking of suing him?"

"That's not how I do things. My daughter is alive, and that's the only thing that matters."

"You won't file a complaint for reparations?"

"I just told you, no!" Benjamin responded.

"You know, you have every right…"

"I have never been litigious. Life is too short, and my time is too valuable to waste it in court."

"Well, then tell me why you're interested in knowing more about Rinetti." Barbaroux insisted.

"I think it's obvious," Benjamin said in barely a whisper. "After what just happened to my daughter, I consider this a very personal matter."

"I repeat, Mr. Cooker, this is a police investigation, and as much as I value your perceptiveness and opinions—and your dumb luck—I don't want you poking around where you don't belong."

4

"Go. I'll be fine." Margaux looked as beautiful as ever, even with her hair mussed and a complexion so pale, it barely contrasted with the white hospital sheets. "Besides, I'm asleep most of the time. I'm not good company."

Benjamin and Elisabeth had just announced they would stay in Bordeaux with her. The friends they had planned to vacation with would have sole use of their rented villa.

"It's out of the question that you languish here in the heat because of me," she insisted.

Elisabeth had finally acquiesced. "As you wish, darling," she said, taking her daughter's hand. "Are you sure you'll be all right?"

"I'll be fine."

Benjamin sighed. "Stubborn and ardent clinging to one's opinion is the best proof of stupidity."

"Michel de Montaigne," Margaux said.

"I see you've come back to your full senses, at least. How could you have gone out with that... that, madman?"

"Papa! Antoine was every bit a gentleman! We had an accident. It wasn't his fault."

"Had he been drinking?"

"You sound like the cops who questioned me. I won't even answer you."

"Benjamin, Margaux, that's enough," Elisabeth said.

Margaux turned to her mother. "Is he going to be okay?"

"He's still in intensive care, darling. We don't know. It doesn't look good."

Margaux turned her head away. They remained silent for several minutes.

"Go," Margaux said.

As they reached the door, she called out, "Papa, I know you'll be coming back to town to work. Come see me."

5

Hoping he could get his mind off the accident, Benjamin stopped to look at the boats. It was one of his simple pleasures. He could stand on a dock or sit on an overturned boat for hours at a time and stare into the haze shrouding the white silhouette of Arcachon. Around the Île aux Oiseaux, swarms of sailboats were gliding over the waves. Farther away, toward the Banc de Bernet, speedboats were growling noisily, disrupting the slow and sinuous dance of the brightly colored fishing vessels whose slender bows were gracefully negotiating the turbulence. A stone's throw from the pier, between the oyster beds, one had to withstand the onslaught of the Jet Skis and water scooters. Benjamin couldn't hide his glee when one of them ran aground on a sandbar or flooded its engine. He felt the same happy vengeance that he experienced when he crushed a mosquito bent on disturbing a peaceful evening.

Benjamin didn't have the soul of a true sailor, but he couldn't live far from the ocean. He often left the tranquility of Grangebelle and the bustle of Bordeaux to go walking along the seashore, even for just an hour. He loved hearing the surf and feeling the spray of the saltwater—alone or with Bacchus gamboling beside him. In his mid-thirties, he had bought himself an Artaban 660, a pretty second-hand colonial-style boat with a white canvas canopy and navy-blue hull. It had the dated elegance of boats that were made between the two world wars. For a few years, Benjamin contentedly sailed along one shore or another in the Arcachon Bay, depending on the temperament of the tides. Then time became scarcer, and he sold the boat to a young radio announcer who daydreamed as much as he did and had a taste for lazy traveling.

He sauntered a bit wearily toward the port of La Vigne and arrived at La Planquette, where Elisabeth was unpacking the suitcases. It was the third year the Cookers were renting this simple villa, designed for idleness and relaxation. They were sharing it with their Parisian friends, Leslie and Ludovic Lamotte, who had fallen in love with the bay and the peninsula. They couldn't imagine being anywhere else in the summer.

Leslie worked for an advertising company that specialized in cosmetics and ready-to-wear apparel. Her work both excited and exhausted her, and she looked forward to devoting her vacations to her children. Victor and Aristide had delicate features and such fair skin, even a raffia beach bag full of sunscreen was hardly sufficient.

Ludovic, who had long blond hair and blue-gray eyes, was an unusual mix of idealism and pragmatism. Benjamin had met him at a sale of rare vintages at the Hôtel Drouot auction house in Paris. They had struck up a friendship while commenting on the exorbitant prices of certain private cellars and had continued their conversation at a little neighborhood brasserie. Ludovic was delighted to find himself in the company of the brilliant winemaker, whose guide he knew well.

After trying his hand at selling old furniture, pop art paintings, and nineteen-seventies memorabilia, Ludovic had finally decided that he was more of an antiquarian than a dealer of bric-a-brac. He changed direction and started searching out rare items from the wine-making world: stamped pewter pitchers, china cabinets from châteaus, wood and metal wine racks, crystal carafes, and hand-blown wine glasses.

Eventually, Ludovic became interested in rare old vintages. Picking up bottles during his travels, he managed to acquire an astonishing reserve of rare finds with faded labels mottled with mold that attested to several decades of storage. This unusual business earned him frequent consultations with billionaires from the United States and Lebanon, a country that had an ancient viticultural region but where popular acceptance of wine drinking was relatively new. Ludovic served as a sort of wine archeologist for these rich clients.

Benjamin, who considered himself more of a taster than a drinker, understood perfectly how Ludovic had happened upon his chosen field. Life was full of back roads and wrong turns. But for the person with vision and passion, those meanderings inevitably led to the right place.

Benjamin always arrived at the coast with suitcases full of wines from his cellar, which he fully enjoyed sharing with his guests. The foursome generally indulged in white wine during their shared vacation. They would have their first glass after returning from the beach in the late afternoon. They had agreed that no one would drink at lunchtime, and this proved to be a wise decision, as the daytime temperature was almost always hovered in the high eighties. When it came to the early evening ritual, Benjamin would offer a Côtes de Gascogne, a Meursault, a Bergerac, or perhaps a Bugey. He also took pleasure in pouring a Puligny-Montrachet, an Entre-Deux-Mers, or a Côtes de Provence. Sometimes he teased his wife and friends by combining prestigious estate vintages with harmoniously structured table wines.

Ludovic, on the other hand, had a sentimental affection for the Carbonnieux he had discovered a few years earlier at a Cap Ferret wine bar. He couldn't imagine a vacation at La Planquette without a case of this amber-colored Pessac-Léognan with mineral properties and a delicate mint bouquet enhanced by fine notes of toasted brioche. He was equally fond of a competitively priced Touraine wine that offered the sauvignon's refreshing qualities and aromatic elegance.

They gathered shrimp, snails, and oysters and ate them with garlic butter and a glass of wine as the waning light of the afternoon sun shimmered through the upper branches of the pine trees. Sometimes they nibbled pistachios, toasted almonds, slices of Aveyron sausage, or slivers of a good Laguiole cheese while watching the children play and preparing a fire for their dinner of red sea bream, marinated mackerel, or tuna.

"If only our everyday lives were this relaxing," Elisabeth sighed, delicately wiping a spot of condensation off her wineglass.

"It feels like we're at the end of the earth," Leslie said quietly. "I can't wait until Margaux can join us."

"When do you expect her to get out of the hospital?" Ludovic asked.

"The doctor wants to keep her a little longer," Benjamin said, uncorking a bottle of Côtes de Saint-Mont, Les Vignes Retrouvées. "But I hate the thought of her alone in Bordeaux. If she hadn't absolutely insisted that we keep our plans, I'd be back there right now. As it is, I feel guilty that we're enjoying ourselves while she's still recovering."

Elisabeth put her glass down and stared at her husband. "Benjamin, I feel guilty too. But you know how stubborn she can be. She wouldn't hear of us staying in Bordeaux, and she can get the rest she needs in the hospital. She's recovering from a trauma, after all."

The Lamottes agreed with Elisabeth and insisted that it was best to trust the doctors, who believed that Margaux needed to remain in the hospital. Benjamin, however, was intractable and grumpy.

"What are they doing for her that we can't? She can get all the rest she needs while staying with us. And Cap Ferret is known for its spa therapy centers. She could regain her health much better here, with our care, the fresh sea air, and all these trees."

He lifted nose and inhaled the aromas of pine resin and the sea to underscore his point.

"The best way to recover and forget the accident is to enjoy life. She can't do that when she's surrounded by the smells of disinfectant and hospital food, along with scores of nurses and doctors interrupting her sleep. She shouldn't be spending her vacation this way. I know my daughter. If she wouldn't let us stay with her, we should have insisted that she come with us, and I could have won her over. Even now I'm willing to march into that hospital and sign the discharge papers myself."

He had gotten carried away. Elisabeth and the Lamottes were staring at him.

"Benjamin, think about it," Elisabeth said, putting her hand on his. "We were willing to stay with her, but Margaux wouldn't have it. She didn't want us to change our plans, and she assured us that she would be perfectly fine in the hospital. She's a grown woman. She has the right to make decisions for herself. Give her some credit."

But Benjamin was still vexed. He got up and decided to take a stroll on the jetty by the docks. Haloed in pink light, the last boats were coming in and slowly tying up. A couple of amateur sailors in their sixties were hosing down their little catamaran while a tanned and muscled young man in a white tank top and kaki shorts was polishing the deck equipment of his Riva. Benjamin pulled out his cell phone and entered a number.

"Good evening, boss. Mission accomplished, but what a tough day!" Virgile's voice was weary.

"Thank you for all that you're doing. We'll take stock tomorrow. Does the name Rinetti mean anything to you?"

"A brand of shoes?" Virgile said. "Pasta, maybe?"

"Stop being an imbecile, Virgile. He was the manager of Gayraud-Valrose."

"The guy who was with your daughter?"

41

"Yes. I'd like to get some information on him. See what you can find out, but be discreet."

"I know the Château Gayraud-Valrose pretty well. I did an internship there when I was in my second year at La Tour Blanche. We could head over there if you want."

"Tell me more, Virgile."

"I said 'pretty well,' but I meant 'very well.' I spent a little more than a month there, and I mostly worked with the vineyard manager. An old guy, not easygoing by any stretch, but a recognized expert: Georges Moncaillou. I'm sure you've heard of him."

"That name does ring a bell."

"I was mostly in the vineyards, but I still got to know the cellar master, Stéphane Sarrazin. I think he's still there. Actually, I'd like to see him again. He was a quite a guy."

"In what way?"

"I might as well confess. He fixed me up with the château's secretary, who was a bit stuck up— the type who knows very well that she's pretty and looks down on you. I don't know how Stéphane did it, but as soon as he walked into a room, all the girls noticed him. He had a knack for making women laugh. Still, he never took advantage. He was a family man and faithful to his wife. At any rate, he introduced me to the secretary, and thanks to his charm, she warmed up to me. Funny, isn't it?"

"Uh-huh." Benjamin smiled. "It seems your internship at Gayraud-Valrose was especially beneficial in the area of women's studies."

"You have no idea."

6

Benjamin took in the château perched above the estate and knew it was exactly what tourists expected to see when they drove along the wine roads of the Médoc. Built in the late nineteenth century, the aristocratic residence of the Gayraud family was situated on a hilltop covered with fine gravel and sandy soil. It was a structure commensurate with the once-powerful family's commercial success. The massive square mansion topped with a slate mansard roof stood at the end of a driveway lined with palm trees and rosebushes, which once grew wild here. Cast-iron Medici vases lined the entry steps, and little windowpanes reflected the green of the surrounding vineyard. The nearby buildings, used for winemaking, had a proud, solid, and graceful allure. Surrounded by ampelopsis shrubs, they blended with the landscape.

The winemaker studied the eroded sculpture of a beautiful disciple of Bacchus, a layer of moss covering her tangle of grapes. Virgile, meanwhile, headed to the wine cellar to look for Stéphane Sarrazin, walking past a man wearing a beret who was squatting next to a moped with a wrench in hand. When Benjamin joined them, the two men were already deep in conversation. Sarrazin greeted Benjamin with a strong handshake.

"I will be with you in two minutes, Mr. Cooker. I just need to give some instructions on topping up the barrels."

Benjamin and his assistant left the building and sought shade under a chestnut tree. It was only ten, but the sun was already beating down. Benjamin missed the sea breeze he'd left behind in Cap Ferret that morning.

"So?" he asked, wiping his forehead with his handkerchief. "Was he surprised to see you?"

"No, I don't think so," Virgile said, shrugging. "At least he didn't say so. It was as if we'd seen each other just yesterday."

They didn't have time say more. Stéphane Sarrazin emerged from the wine cellar. He motioned to them to wait where they were and joined them under the tree. Benjamin guessed that he was in his forties, and he was still a handsome man: average height, rather slim, short slightly graying hair, broad forehead, bushy eyebrows, and playful eyes. But his somewhat weary gait and nonchalant bearing suggested underlying disappointment. No bitterness or regret, but an awareness of pain.

"From your description yesterday, I was expecting a more jovial-looking man," Benjamin said.

"Well, they've just gotten some unsettling news, boss. But it's true, I remember that Sarrazin could be cold sometimes, and he didn't have any illusions about people."

"I've come to see you on unofficial business, Mr. Sarrazin," Benjamin said when the cellar master reached them. "You probably know why I'm here."

The man sized up Benjamin with amused eyes. He didn't seem the slightest bit fazed to find himself in the company of one of France's best-known wine experts. Courteous, respectful, and full of himself, Benjamin was thinking.

"Virgile mentioned that he knew you," Benjamin continued. "So I've taken the liberty to come see you. I hope you will forgive the interruption."

Stéphane Sarrazin grinned ever so slightly. The small wrinkles at the corners of his eyes accentuated his impertinent look.

"No need to beat around the bush, Mr. Cooker. You want to know about Antoine Rinetti."

"Absolutely. I assume you know that his condition is serious."

"Of course. He works here. The château is in touch with the hospital. And I do read the *Sud-Ouest*, like everyone else, so I also know that your daughter was in the car."

"Do you think someone may have wanted to harm him?"

"Why are you asking?"

Benjamin took out his handkerchief and wiped his brow.

"I might as well tell you right away what the newspapers will be reporting. His car was sabotaged."

Virgile, who had been standing off to the side, stepped in and joined the conversation. Benjamin sensed that the cellar master's grin, verging on smug, was starting to annoy his assistant.

"That his car may have been sabotaged doesn't seem to surprise you," Virgile said.

"Not really."

"Or bother you," Benjamin added.

"You've gotten straight to the point with me, so I'll level with you. The accident didn't upset me much."

"Even though he's the château manager, and you worked together every day?"

"I'm not very good at playacting, so I'll just tell you: since Rinetti has been here, we've had some changes that were difficult to swallow."

"I'm not asking you to betray the trust of your employers, but maybe you could enlighten me about…"

"My code of silence is relative," Sarrazin interrupted. "Beyond our winemaking techniques, I am free to speak my mind, and I can tell you what everyone else is thinking."

Sarrazin began talking about the estate, and while he had promised to be candid, he chose his words carefully, measuring his allusions and calculating the effects of surprise. Some of his pointed remarks seemed to have hidden meanings Benjamin couldn't make out. Sarrazin winked at Virgile when he spoke of an old employee or certain aspects of the property's operations. At times, the winemaker wondered whether Sarrazin was joking or serious. On the whole, though, what Benjamin heard was a cautionary exposé.

The last heir of the Gayraud family had made some bad investments and suffered setbacks related to the mismanagement of the estate. A legal battle to resolve a contested inheritance had finally worn out the man, who wasn't even a direct descendent of the original founders. He was forced to sell the property to avoid bankruptcy. At the beginning of the year, Helvetica-Sûr, an insurance company from Bâle, had acquired the estate for a relatively paltry sum. People in the area said the land had been sold off for a gulp of wine, and since this pitiful transaction, no one had seen Gayraud.

"Indeed, I've never run into him in Bordeaux," Benjamin said.

Stéphane Sarrazin didn't acknowledge this remark. He continued. The insurance company quickly examined the books and hired experts to provide an accurate assessment. They recommended bringing in an administrator to restore order. The company saw fit to appoint a young man trained in statistical analysis and austerity marketing. Antoine Rinetti had arrived in April, and the following day, he took draconian measures. He slashed overhead and operating budgets. He knew nothing about the winemaking world. He had never set foot in a wine cellar or a vineyard, and he had no interest in learning. His mind was made up: the estate would be managed like a manufacturing company that turned out gizmos.

"Then one day, Rinetti called everyone into the reception room," Sarrazin said.

"Which room?" Virgile asked. "The one with the cherubs and flowers on the ceiling? You know, where you introduced me to that beauty?"

Sarrazin gave Virgile a dull look and went on. "He was so arrogant. He said yields were too low and production costs and salaries were too high. We needed to amortize investments, communicate more, and upgrade our image. He kept going on and on about what was wrong. Then he looked us in the eye, one after the other, and promised he'd turn the château into an efficient business in no time."

"Clearly, he's not from the wine world," Benjamin said.

"He made it clear that he intended to stanch the flow of red ink, and he would begin with the payroll. He would keep the steward, Phillipe Cazevielle, and me. But two laborers and an assistant cellar master would be let go. He was almost cheerful about it. Interns or temporary workers, depending on seasonal needs, would take their place. Finally, he announced that Georges Moncaillou, the vineyard manager, would be afforded—in other words forced to take—an early retirement at the age of fifty-seven. No one dared to question him. We went our separate ways without a word. I'm surprised Rinetti didn't deduct the half hour we were in there with him from our paychecks."

"What happened then?" Virgile asked. "Did he implement the changes immediately?"

"The next day, Georges Moncaillou committed suicide: a shotgun blast to the neck. He was a hunter, you know."

"Shit, Moncaillou!" Virgile nearly shouted. "Fucking shit!"

The cellar master was quiet for a moment, clenching his jaw in a seeming attempt to contain his emotion. Benjamin couldn't tell whether Sarrazin was suppressing grief or anger. He then spoke briefly about the funeral, when the residents of the town and employees of neighboring châteaus in the Margaux appellation came together. Antoine Rinetti had even had the gall to show up.

"What about Moncaillou's son?" Virgile asked.

"Gilles? Oh, he's still working for the estate, kowtowing morning and night, just like he always has."

"It must be tough on him," Benjamin said.

"He doesn't show it, but he's taken to wearing his father's threadbare beret out in the vineyards. There's no telling what's brewing in his head."

"Who's managing the vineyard now?" Benjamin asked.

"A man named Francis Gardel, from the Charente in the Cognac area. He's nothing like old Georges."

"Boss, Moncaillou was one of the good ones," Virglile said. "He'd served Gayraud-Valrose for, what, thirty years? And he'd done tons to improve the state of the vines."

"He was really passionate about terroir. He made replanting, irrigation, and soil improvement an art form. He's sorely missed," Sarrazin said. "Here at Valrose, there are more thorns than petals these days."

Sarrazin seemed ready to walk away. But instead, he looked Benjamin in the eye.

"You know, Mr. Cooker, you judged us harshly in the latest edition of your guide."

"Not really. I was actually full of praise for your last two prestige vintages."

"That's true, but you criticized the tannins. I believe your words were 'unpredictable extraction,' if I remember correctly."

"I think they shouldn't have been so pronounced. They should have been better blended and fuller."

"Everyone here was complaining about you when the guide came out. But I have to admit that I agreed, more or less, with your assessment. That's just between us, of course."

"Of course. My silence in that regard goes without saying," Benjamin replied.

They shook hands with the firm grip of men who honor the soil, the grapes, the art of winemaking, and the labors of those who worked the vineyards.

In the distance, the convertible, parked near a clump of old rosebushes, gleamed in the sun. Not a hint of cloud disrupted the sky. Seagulls were flying overhead, carried on the warm currents floating above the river.

"I didn't expect him to be such a talker," Benjamin said.

"Why do you say that?" Virgile asked.

"Because he's cynical and intelligent. He doubts everything and believes in no one. But beneath that façade, there's a kind of desperation. I wouldn't be surprised if he had a violent streak."

"It sounded to me like he wanted to justify the pronounced tannins," Virgile said, with a shrug.

"Do you think so? I don't know. There something in his eyes...something kind of borderline."

"Oh, he's not crazy. I can assure you of that," Virgile said. "He's too self-contained."

"That's precisely what worries me."

7

It hadn't rained in seven weeks. According to the news, the drought was beginning to concern government officials, but not the ones who counted. The prime minister made an effort to sound reassuring but couldn't hide his annoyance at being disturbed during his vacation. His pat phrases sounded more paternalistic than encouraging. He advised patience. Yet farmers were already complaining about a severe shortage of feed for their livestock. Grain fields were withering under the sun. Even more serious, brownouts were beginning to affect the elderly in nursing homes and newborns who hadn't yet developed the ability to sweat.

"Animals, babies, and old people. They just might bring down the government," Benjamin said as he parked in front of 46 Allées de Tourny.

He turned the radio off and kept the engine running.

"I'm not getting out, Virgile. I have some things to tend to. We'll meet up in the early afternoon."

"And what should I do in the meantime?"

"Everything I had planned to do myself, plus your own work that's still not done. Ask Jacqueline for the mail. Take care of what's urgent, and only answer the estates whose issues we handle. Just a few words telling them we received their inquiries. That will keep them calm for a few days. Then schedule the visits for the coming weeks. Call the owners to inform them of our arrival, and block out the times. Contact the Beaujolais Wine Council, and make sure they send us absolutely every tasting sample before the end of August. Then stop by the lab and check with Alexandrine to see where we are with the leaf analyses from the Premieres Côtes de Bordeaux and Entre-deux-Mers. Oh, I forgot—organize the last studies we did on the soil, and tell the Léognan estates that we will continue our field investigations to-morrow or the day after. That should be enough for you to handle."

"In other words, you want me to do the work of two people in three hours, tops."

"Two and a half if you take time for lunch." Benjamin winked at his assistant and glanced in his rearview mirror before merging with the traffic.

Benjamin waved to Virgile. He felt the hot air rising from the pavement as he made his way toward the Place Gambetta, where he headed west on the Rue Judaïque. Arriving at Pellegrin

Hospital, he parked under the meager shade of a linden tree and hurried into the lobby. He shivered in the air conditioning, which was set too low. The heat wave was putting too much demand on the power grid. The winemaker understood that surgical facilities and some patient rooms needed to be cool, but keeping the whole hospital this cold was foolhardy. Why hospital administrators didn't realize this was beyond Benjamin, but he had other priorities today. He hurried toward Margaux's room, excited at the prospect of treating his daughter to a lovely surprise. He climbed the stairs two at a time, finally reaching her floor. Almost slipping on the shiny linoleum, he entered her room without knocking, a bit winded but in a good mood.

"My little angel, we're breaking out!"

"Are you kidnapping me?" Margaux burst out laughing.

"Yes, that's right. It's an abduction, and the stagecoach will be here in less than ten minutes!"

Benjamin paused, suddenly realizing that his daughter was sitting in a visitor's chair and dressed in her street clothes. A pair of crutches was leaning against one of the armrests, and a small cloth bag was at her feet.

"I already know, Papa. The whole crew at La Planquette called this morning to warn me. They asked me to talk you out of your plan. Maman, Leslie, and Ludovic were worried."

"And so?"

"I told them that you've always had excellent ideas. Maman was furious. She said that neither of us have ever listened to her, and between a stubborn husband and a capricious daughter, she would never have the last word. I let the storm pass, and five minutes later—you know her—she seemed agreeable. I think she's actually relieved that I'll be closer. She'll be able to keep an eye on me."

"I am sure she's already prepared a wonderful room for you and everything's ready for your arrival. Here, sign the discharge papers."

"The doctor has already come by and given me my instructions. He groaned a bit and said I'd be better off if I stayed in the hospital's rehab unit, but I think he understood. And, of course, I'll need to see the orthopedic surgeon for a follow-up."

"I'll send the doctor a case of good wine. That will make him happy," Benjamin said, picking up Margaux's bag. "Okay, off we go. I still have some work to do today, with the heat wave and all, so I've got a taxi waiting outside to whisk you to La Planquette. I've also hired a nurse to ride with you and help you settle in your room."

The nurse poked her head through the half-open door, and together they helped Margaux through the hospital and into the waiting taxi. Benjamin kissed his daughter's forehead and promised to join everyone at La Planquette later.

He walked over to his Mercedes, and as soon as he slipped behind the wheel, he felt his cell phone vibrate in his pocket. He heard the raspy voice of Inspector Barbaroux when he put it to his ear.

"So, Mr. Cooker, I see you're not wasting any time!"

"News travels fast. I guess you stopped by at Gayraud-Valrose?"

"Right after your visit," Barbaroux said. "I told you to leave it alone, and now you're one move ahead of me!" The inspector laughed, but it sounded forced. Benjamin could tell he was irritated.

"It's not a chess game, Inspector."

"Who's talking about chess? We'd do better if we worked together."

"Do you have any news?"

"Do you?"

"If we keep up this little game, we'll just go around in circles," Benjamin said. Now he was getting annoyed.

"So let's put our cards on the table. That way we'll both win."

"I spoke with Stéphane Sarrazin," Benjamin said, quickly summarizing the interview with the cellar master, keeping his impressions of the man's singular personality to himself. He was not inclined to reveal his gut instincts to someone whose profession encouraged suspicion.

"Bottom line," Barbaroux interrupted, "you haven't made any more progress than I have. I got more or less the same information going through other channels. And it would seem to make all those disgruntled workers potential suspects, wouldn't it?"

"At any rate, it will be difficult for me get onto the Gayraud-Valrose property for any length of time, as I have no official role in the investigation, and I've never done any work for them. I'm familiar with their production, but my only tie with the estate is the fact that my daughter almost died because of their new manager. Well, because of someone who wanted to do away with him."

"By the way, Mr. Cooker, it seems that you are not in the good graces of Gayraud-Valrose."

"Why do you say that?"

"Naturally, the subject of your daughter came up when I was asking about Rinetti and the accident. In the course of the conversation, I heard some opinions about you."

"Opinions?"

"Yes. Commonly held, by the way."

"Come on, Inspector. Spill the beans. I can sense that you're dying to tell me."

"I got the impression that you roasted them in your last guide."

"I stand by every word in my review. Their tannins should have been more carefully extracted."

Barbaroux had been studying oenology for more than a year. He had signed up for a tasting course and had never missed a class. In addition, he was beginning to acquire an impressive cellar by following the recommendations in the *Cooker Guide*. The inspector's newfound passion had created a rather unexpected relationship between the two of them. Despite some differences of opinion, Benjamin and he had developed a measure of trust, and the winemaker was aware that their association stroked the inspector's ego.

"I haven't tasted that wine," Barbaroux admitted. "But from what you wrote, I also got the impression that it lacked a long finish."

"What are you getting at?"

"I might as well tell you. I questioned the steward, Philippe Cazevielle, and he didn't have anything complimentary to say about you. I believe he used the words 'dictator of good taste,' and 'pope without a palace.' He's obviously a very touchy kind of guy, and he doesn't take kindly to criticism of the work they do at the château. I don't really think you were the target of the accident your daughter was in, but who knows?"

"I don't buy that. I already told you, anyone who reads my guide knows that my evaluations are subjective but considered and fair. I've spent my life establishing my reputation in this profession, and even when I've come off as a bit harsh, I can't remember anyone holding a grudge. If every estate criticized in my guide reacted that way, I'd have to get a bodyguard."

"You can never be too careful, Mr. Cooker."

"Someone who's angry with me over what I've written in one of my guide can find other ways to ruin my life. I'm sorry, Inspector, but I think you're being a bit too cynical, even paranoid. I think Antoine Rinetti was targeted. My daughter just happened to be in the car."

"Perhaps. But let's not overlook any possibility. As far as Rinetti is concerned, I got some interesting intelligence from a few colleagues in the Côte d'Azur. He's a pretty complicated character. He's from a well-known but penniless family in Nice, was a good student in high school, had leftist leanings in college prep school, majored in math at the university, and graduated with honors. In short, nothing much stands out up to that point."

"Yes," Benjamin said. "He sounds rather ordinary."

"That changed when a British financial firm hired him as a researcher. His particular area was applied statistics. Rinetti devised a highly efficient management-control system adapted to the stock market. He earned the firm a lot of dough. When I say a lot, I mean a downright huge amount."

Barbaroux cleared his throat and continued. "After he'd been with the firm for three years, the Brits opened an office near Nice, and they made him director of research. The new job had an obscenely high salary and all the perks a rising star could lust for: stock options, a Ferrari, eighty-seven employees, a secretary recruited from the Élite agency, and an unbelievable expense account."

"Hmm. He's still sounding ordinary. An ordinary person with money," But Benjamin was clenching his jaw. Money couldn't give a man substance, and a man of substance was what he expected for his daughter.

"So Rinetti was living the high life, Barbaroux continued. And he started hanging out with all the crème de la crème between Cannes and Monaco. You know what that means down there. He made the inevitable acquaintance of members of the Italian mafia, crooked investors, stinking rich cougars, and casino sharks. They were looking for places to hide their money—both dirty and clean—and he was the man who could help them. He became indispensable, creating sham companies in Ventimiglia, Luxembourg, Panama, and Ireland. And before long, everyone was relying on him."

"All that to end up in the Médoc?" Benjamin said.

"I haven't finished. With all the dinners at the private clubs and the parties on Lebanese yachts, he soon became a collector of Monaco heiresses and thousand-euro hookers."

Benjamin was grinding his teeth now. "Ordinary, I tell you." The worst kind of ordinary.

"Then he made the big mistake. He seduced a lonely Swedish woman fond of visiting a spa near Nice. She happened to be the company president's wife. That was the beginning of the end for him. The English gave him a closer look and found out that he was up to his eyeballs in shady business. He was forced to resign—no golden parachute, no nothing. But he landed on his feet. One of his old leftist pals heads up a large Swiss-based insurance company, Helvetica-Sûr, and hired him."

"That still doesn't explain how he wound up in a vineyard in Bordeaux," Benjamin insisted.

"The insurance company figured it was best to have him lie low for a while, at least until his problems in Nice died down. When the company invested in the vineyard, as they all do these days, they figured it was a good place to park him until he could take up where he left off. The assignment was supposed to be temporary. Their long-term goal was to have him take care of the big clients. And there's no disputing that he excelled at that. He just got burned because he bedded the wrong woman."

Barbaroux went quiet. Benjamin couldn't even speak. He was remembering how Rinetti had looked at his daughter, how he had so casually whispered in her ear.

"You still there?" the inspector asked.

Benjamin shook himself. "Given what you've just told me, it's possible that his car was sabotaged by someone who had nothing to do with the vineyard. A person from his former life may have wanted to settle a score."

"You're right. That is a possibility. At any rate, I contacted the police departments in Nice and nearby communities to see what they can find. And I'm looking into every employee and former employee at the château. How is your daughter doing?"

"She's better, Inspector," Benjamin responded. "And she's in a safe place."

Benjamin felt the anger surge again as he ended the call. "And to think that Margaux could have fallen into the scoundrel's clutches," he muttered.

8

Benjamin was stunned by the amount of work Virgile had done in less than two hours. He congratulated him with an affectionate pat on the back.

"I hope you at least took time to eat."

"I had a glass of Lillet blanc with olives—pitted, to save time."

"I didn't think you were going to do everything on my list. I was joking."

"I knew that, boss. But better to get it out of the way. And to be honest, at least it's almost cool here. I prefer doing this to inspecting the Léognan vineyards."

"They're predicting ninety-seven degrees tomorrow. I'm with you. I'd rather be here than there." Benjamin took out a handkerchief and mopped his forehead. Then he draped the hankie over the back of a chair to let it dry out.

"It sounds like the heat wave is claiming victims all over France," Virgile said. "Jacqueline told me that they found an old man dead in the building next door. His apartment didn't have any air conditioning. He'd been gone for three days before a niece showed up to check on him. How many other elderly people are in the same boat? No air conditioning or forced to choose being staying cool and having food to eat. It's terrible."

"If the weather doesn't break soon, I'm afraid we're headed for a national disaster."

"Still, it's strange. There are countries that are hotter than ours where old people don't die because of the temperature. Take Ethiopia, for example, and Mexico."

"That's not exactly true, Virgile. Anyone who's exposed to extreme heat is vulnerable. But people who live in very hot climates do adapt to an extent. Their blood concentrations of water and salt, for example, adjust to allow greater cooling. And the people in these regions have adjusted their lifestyles, doing their hard work during the coolest parts of the day, sleeping in the afternoon and staying awake long into the night. In this sense, the great Marcel was wrong when he said our habits accompany us even into places where they serve no useful purpose.

"Who is this great Marcel?"

"Proust, a writer who knew what he was talking about."

"I know who he was, thank you. I'm not illiterate. He's the dude who for a long time would go to bed early so that he could write all night long. He tried to get in with the aristocracy and coughed up blood. I don't think his stuff is badly written. It just gives me a headache."

Benjamin smiled at his assistant. He hoped the boy would never change. Unaffected, reliable, straightforward, and more sensitive than he would like to appear, Virgile was invaluable. He was a rare individual whose mind was still unfettered by propriety. He was quick to understand, did not worry about moral or cultural dictates, always adjusted to the most extreme situations, spoke with irony, and maintained mischievous silence. He had a peasant's common sense that allowed him to avoid any traps set for him. It was a godsend to have a young man of his caliber working for Cooker & Co.

They decided to go to the laboratory, where Alexandrine de la Palussière was probably awaiting them. They went down the Allées de Tourny and walked past the Grand-Théâtre and the Cours du Chapeau-Rouge, finally arriving in a sweat in front of a building whose peeling façade needed a good facelift. They took the elevator, and Benjamin pulled out a clean handkerchief embroidered with his initials. He wiped his forehead while Virgile looked on with a smirk on his face.

"Yes, my boy, there are still old fools who use cloth handkerchiefs, even cloth handkerchiefs with monograms. I have my own little habits, which do, indeed, serve a purpose."

When they entered the lab, a clearly impatient and distressed Alexandrine de la Palussière pointed to a pile of documents on her desk. She shook her employer's hand and gave Virgile a nod.

"I was anxious to see you," she said. "There are many signs of dehydration on the samples you brought me. Some of the estates also have parasites. The treatments in those vineyards need to be stepped up. My reports are on the desk."

"But the pesticides we're using should be lasting longer than usual," Virgile said. "There hasn't been any rain to wash them away. We've been treating the vines about every fourteen days."

Alexandrine spoke directly to Benjamin, ignoring Virgile entirely. "The heat is stressing the vines and making them more vulnerable to infestation. You should be treating the vines every eleven to twelve days."

"We still have time to act on this," Benjamin said. "I'm becoming very concerned about this year's harvest. Even if the vines manage to fend off the parasites, I fear the grapes will be too small and have too much sugar. You know as well as I do that the Institut national des appellations d'origine strictly regulates watering."

"Yeah, but no matter what INAO says, some winemakers will be tempted to break the rules," Virgile cut in.

"We need to send up prayers for rain," Benjamin concluded.

They spent the rest of the afternoon going through the reports Alexandrine had prepared and arranging a schedule for the coming days in order to deal with the most urgent cases. With the help of the biologist, they fine-tuned the treatments for several properties and discussed in detail the most efficient strategies to protect the vineyards from insects and spiders. Benjamin was aware that many estate owners wished they hadn't done their usual hand-thinning of the grapes. But how could they have foreseen this heat wave? It was too late to do anything about that now. They had to deal with their present situation—and quickly. That, and rely on the grace of God.

As Alexandrine was agreeing with the strategy they had mapped out, Benjamin noticed Virgile's eyes wandering from the reports to Alexandrine's white blouse, with its top two buttons undone. He understood. Alexandrine, who had green eyes, an upturned nose, and auburn hair always held back with a mother-of-pearl headband was both good-looking and smart. But Virgile was well aware that Alexandrine had no romantic interest in men. Benjamin suppressed a smile. His assistant obviously saw no harm in looking.

Emerging from the lab, the winemaker and his assistant cowered under the harsh glare of the sun.

The sodden air immediately glued their clothes to their skin.

"I have a favor to ask you, boss," Virgile ventured.

"After the day you've put in, how could I refuse? Unless, of course, it's about a raise."

"Well, it's sort of connected, but not really, either."

"Now you're starting to worry me," Benjamin said, once again wiping his face with his handkerchief.

"Okay, here goes: I have this idea, but I need your help. Would you have time for me right now?"

"You're being awfully careful, Virgile. Go ahead. Jump in with both feet. That's my advice, especially in this weather."

"All right. That's what I'll do. Boss, we've spent a lot of time together, and I think you've passed some of your obsessions on to me."

"And just how have I infected you?" The wine-maker asked.

"I've already picked up the cigar habit, and I'm enjoying it. Well, okay, I'm not smoking your big rough Cubans, but I do like to light up a Dominican now and then."

"It's a very forgivable vice. I would even say commendable."

"With all due respect, I don't share your taste in clothes. Too traditional and British for me. But on the other hand, you've converted me to vintage cars. I can't stand new cars. Too much plastic, and they all look the same: insipid and tasteless. In short, you have really given me a taste for old cars."

"Is that so?"

"Yes. I've been thinking of buying a collector's car for some time now, and I think I've found a gem. But I would like your opinion before I go ahead."

"And where is this car?"

"In town, not very far from here. If you have the time, I'd like you to take a look."

Benjamin and Virgile picked up the convertible on the Allées de Tourny. They drove toward Place de la Victoire and down the Cours de la Somme, one of the gloomiest thoroughfares in Bordeaux. They emerged on Place Nansouty, its usually lush flowerbeds scorched by the sun, and then strayed into one-way streets before finally arriving at a shabby garage adjacent to an old pasta factory that had been turned into artist workshops. The lively street was lined with well-maintained vendor's stalls, including makeshift barbecues. Several neighborhood residents ranging in age from toddler to grandparent were celebrating someone's birthday.

"Boss, I have to warn you. It's a bit unusual here. This is the craziest neighborhood in the city!"

"I feel like I've just arrived at a gypsy feast. Leave it to you to sniff out a place like this, Virgile."

"You ain't seen nothing yet. I want to introduce you to Stofa, the garage owner," Virgile said, walking toward a man in overalls who was poking the embers of a grill. In the light of the fire his tanned skin resembled beautiful Cordoba leather.

"Well, hello, Virgile! You're just in time. Your car is ready. Salem spent the afternoon cleaning it."

"I came with my boss," Virgile said, gesturing to Benjamin, who was hovering close by and felt a bit lost in this country-fair atmosphere in the heart of Bordeaux.

The winemaker shook Stofa's hand and looked him in the eye. The man had the bearing of a Tuareg prince. He bore a striking resemblance to Thelonious Monk. Margaux had all of Monk's albums, and even though Benjamin wasn't a jazz aficionado, he enjoyed listening to them with her. Stofa led them to the back of the garage, where a handsome admiral-blue Peugeot 403 stood gleaming. The body had no scratches or dents. A stylized lion's head graced the radiator grille, and the red leather upholstery was in impeccable condition.

"What year?" Benjamin said, sliding his hand over the body.

"It's a 1959, seven horse power, fifty-three thousand miles on the odometer, one owner. Runs like clockwork." Stofa started the engine and then walked to the front of the car and lifted the hood. "Just listen to that."

Benjamin leaned over and admired the robust simplicity of the engine. "Nineteen fifty-nine. A very good year—at least for Bordeaux wines!"

"I don't know much about booze, but I can tell you that it was a good year for the Peugeot 403. And your assistant here got a real bargain."

"How much?" Benjamin asked, feeling a bit like a horse trader.

"Forty-four hundred euros, believe it or not! A Peugeot 403 is rare nowadays. Columbo, the detective Peter Falk played in the American TV series, drove one of these."

"Indeed, it does appear to be a good price," the winemaker agreed. He turned to Virgile. "If I were you, I wouldn't hesitate. She's a beauty!"

Benjamin sniffed the leather seats and thought of his maternal grandfather, Eugène, who drove along the banks of the Gironde behind the wheel of a Peugeot 403 black station wagon with a roof rack and brakes that squealed at every stop sign.

"I think this car will make you very happy, Virgile."

"I'm glad you like it. I'll seriously consider it."

"If you're concerned about your finances, it's silly not to tell me," Benjamin said. He reached into his jacket to take out his checkbook. "I'll advance you the money, and you can pay me back two hundred dollars a month. Remember to tell Jacqueline to deduct it from your paycheck."

"Are you serious, boss?"

"Do I look like I'm joking? No need to thank me. I'll get the selfish pleasure of seeing you drive this little beauty."

"Let's drink to that," Stofa bellowed, grabbing a bottle of pastis from Salem's hands. "Come join the party. It's a birthday."

He led them to a large room adjacent to the garage, where tables were filled with grilled and roasted pork belly, sausages, and chicken thighs and bowls of pasta, rice, couscous, and french fries. Every resident of the neighborhood, it seemed, had contributed to the lavish buffet. Stofa poured the pastis into glasses lined up on one of the tables.

Benjamin quaffed his Pernod Ricard and didn't balk when his glass was filled again. He couldn't help grinning when he saw the astonished look on his assistant's face.

"Boss, I never thought I'd be seeing you downing pastis," Virgile whispered. "You're very unpredictable."

"Well, it is the national drink, Virgile, after wine, that is."

Intoxicating aromas were beginning to swirl all around the winemaker: anise, red wine, roasted pistachios, garlic sausage, and charcoal. Meanwhile, people were streaming into the room, introducing themselves as they arrived. Lionel, Stéphanie, Pierre, Pauline, Sébastien, Céline, Gilles, Françoise, Léon, Sophie, Jean-Pierre, Daniel, Marguerite, Didier, Bill, Rapido,

Kamel, Virginie, Lolo, and Paillasse. Benjamin shook hands and smiled, knowing very well that he would never remember so many names. But for each and every one, he had a gracious greeting. He was a man who appreciated hospitality, wherever it was extended.

Someone handed him a plastic cup filled with rosé—probably Stéphanie, or was it Pauline? And everyone began to sing golden oldies from the sixties to the accompaniment of an impromptu little band: the teacher on guitar, the writer on bass, the doctor on accordion, and the plumber on harmonica.

Benjamin and Virgile were still there at midnight, their speech a bit muddled and their gait unsteady. They were talking about everything and nothing: cars, rugby, hunting, past carousing, childhood memories, and improbable plans. The air was mild, and a welcome breeze from the sea had finally extinguished the fiery daytime heat.

"What a satisfying evening," Benjamin sighed, lifting his slightly flushed face toward the inky sky studded with stars.

"The spicy merguez sausage, tabouleh, olives, and chilled rosé," Virgile said. "I feel like I've been on an exotic vacation in the Middle East."

"Don't try to cajole me into agreeing to a vacation, Virgile," the winemaker said, his voice a tinge thick. "I'm well aware that you need a break, but this is no time to take off."

"That's not what I meant, boss."

"If you really want to see the ocean, I have an idea, my boy. You can come with me to Cap Ferret tonight. I'm a bit plastered, I admit, and I'd rather not drive. Give me a ride in your Peugeot 403."

"Now? At this hour? I'm not exactly sober myself."

"I've been watching you, Virgile. You haven't kept up with me."

Benjamin walked unsteadily toward the Peugeot, cracked open the door, and flopped into the backseat.

"Come on. Show me what this car of yours made of!"

He stretched out his legs, clasped his hands behind his neck, gave a blissful smile, and immediately fell asleep.

9

Could anyone be hungry enough to eat such an ugly fish? Thick dull-colored flesh, large flat body, fleshy lips that looked almost human. The grey triggerfish seemed to come straight from the imagination of an animated film whose aim was scaring children. Benjamin examined it for a moment, turning it over and evaluating it with a look of disgust. He decided to throw it back into the sea. The two little striped bass, a mullet, and some small fish that they had already caught would be enough to fry up.

Ludovic was quiet, fixed on the red and white floater on his line. Benjamin usually loved these calm interludes when he didn't need to talk, when the landscape was still asleep, and everything seemed renewed. But today, between the rolling of the fishing boat, which made his stomach churn, and a throbbing headache—vestiges of the previous night—the winemaker felt wan and spent.

"You don't look too good," Ludovic said.

"To tell the truth, I feel like my brain's sloshing around in the kelp. I got my cup filled a few too many times last night."

"When I found you snoozing in the back of that vintage car this morning, I almost didn't wake you up. But hey, you've been promising me this fishing trip for a long time, and I figured it would do you some good."

"It was quite an evening," Benjamin said. "Good people who loved talking, singing, and sharing their food and drink. And what a spread it was—a feast, really. They made me feel right at home."

"So where's the car come from?"

"Oh, that's Virgile's new vehicle, the reason behind the expedition that led us to the festivities."

The two of them decided it was time to head back. They dismantled their fishing rods, hung up the lines, and started returning to shore. But it was slow going. The motor began to sputter and spit black plumes of smoke. By the time they reached La Vigne, the boat was moving in fits and starts. They had to restart the motor several times before they could tie up at the dock. Ludovic was upset and anxious to get the boat serviced as soon as possible. The middle of August was a bad time for a breakdown.

After stopping at the market near the light-house, they arrived at La Planquette with a bag of pastries and fresh baguettes. When Benjamin pushed open the garden gate, he could hear Margaux laughing on the terrace. He walked around the corner and found her sitting at the table with Virgile. The two were drinking coffee.

"Papa, you never told me about Virgile's sense of humor. If he ever decides to quit working for you, he could have a future as a comic!"

"Is that so?" Benjamin grumbled, making no effort to conceal his irritation.

"Hello, Mr. Cooker. Did you sleep well?" Virgile asked, lowering his eyes.

"I'm wondering what was so hilarious. I could hear you laughing all the way from the jetty."

"Oh, it's a secret," Margaux whispered, batting her eyes. "Isn't it, Virgile?"

Virgile was plainly ill at ease. He rubbed the stubble on his chin, cleared his throat, and pretended to be interested in the label on the jar of jam in front of him: "oranges, sugar, gelling agent, pectin. Fifty grams of fruit and forty-five grams of sugar for every one hundred grams."

"I see you haven't wasted any time getting to know each other," Benjamin said, pouring himself a cup of coffee because there was no tea.

"I admit that I was very surprised when I found this young man lying on the couch, snoring away," Margaux said, putting her hand on Virgile's arm. Benjamin thought she was being entirely too perky. "It was a nice surprise. You and Maman have told me so much about him."

Virgile's cheeks were turning pink. He continued to read the label on the jam. "Calories: 183. Protein: 0.4 grams. Carbohydrates: 45 grams. Lipids: 0.1 gram. Fiber: 1 gram. Sodium: 3.3 grams."

"Can we take off when you've found the expiration date, Virgile? We have a lot of work today."

"Do you want to go right away?"

"Yes. I just need to take a shower, and then we're off."

On the road to Bordeaux, they hardly spoke to each other. Benjamin mumbled sullenly in response to Virgile's offhanded remarks. The winemaker was annoyed with himself for reacting this way. He had only himself to blame. If he hadn't been in such bad shape the night before, Margaux wouldn't have met his assistant.

Too handsome, too clever, and obviously too funny, Virgile was a fox in the henhouse. All the more dangerous because his daughter apparently had a weakness for charmers. He hadn't been aware of this trait before her flirtation with Antoine Rinetti. Benjamin was feeling a twinge of jealousy. But it was more than jealousy. His daughter was in a vulnerable state and needed to be protected. Even if Virgile's intentions were honorable—and he had reason to question that, based on his experience with the young man—a model assistant didn't necessarily make an ideal son-in-law.

As they approached the first vines of Léognan, Virgile slid open the 403's sunroof and ventured a comment that helped to lighten the mood.

"I took a look at your white wines at La Planquette. Are you angry with the Alsatians?"

"On the contrary, you know how much I love Alsace whites. I only go there three or four days a year to taste them on site, but they're memorable, believe me."

"I thought so," Virgile said. "And I thought you had quite a few of them in your cellar."

"Good observation," Benjamin said. "I didn't bring any to La Planquette. We have so many great wines in the Southwest."

"I did see some Touraine, though."

"That was Ludovic. Oh, I grabbed a few Côtes de Beaune, but I wish I had brought some selections from Alsace, which can be quite magnificent."

The winemaker stretched out his legs and sank deeper in his leather seat. He launched into a discourse on the way Pfaffenheim and Gueberschwihr wines were improving and the strong personality of Loew estate riesling. Then there was the pinot gris produced by the Domaines Schlumberger, whose cuvée Les Princes Abbés he particularly enjoyed. The list didn't stop there: André Ostertag's old-vine sylvaner had sophisticated elegance, and Richard Auther produced a perfectly fermented grand cru Winzenberg riesling.

"I have a weakness for gewurztraminers," Virgile managed to get in.

"Oh, then you'll love the late harvests from the Rolly Gassmann estate, which are exceptional in every way, and the excellent cuvée Laurence produced by the Weinbach estate."

"I don't even know where that is. All I know about Alsace I learned in high-school geography—I can locate Strasbourg and Colmar on a map, and know the highest spot in the Vosges mountains: the Grand Ballon of Guebwiller. But all those names full of consonants do me in: Rorsh-whatever, Ep-who-knows, and Pfaff-choom."

"Make an effort, boy. Use those neurons of yours: that would be Rorschwihr, Epfig, and Pfaffenheim. And please don't forget Westhoffen and Kaysersberg. Someday I will take you there, and you will see that it's serious wine country."

Benjamin and Virgile slipped into a world that was theirs alone whenever they discussed bottles, labels, vintages, and the infinite range of aromas and textures. There, all worries and disagreements vanished. Grievances dissolved in the heady vapors of wine. Virgile knew this perfectly well, and he was cleverly and delicately bringing about a reconciliation with his employer. The image of Margaux, which had interfered with their usual camaraderie, slowly faded. Soon they were discussing grape varieties, alluvial deposits, fermentation, and wines to age.

Despite the brutal sun bleaching the earth, the morning unfolded in almost unhoped-for serenity. Even though they were working hard in the heat, their minds were at peace. They were able to accomplish an impressive amount of work in just a few hours. Shortly after noon, however, Benjamin grew weary of walking the rows of vines and suggested that they take a break and have a quick lunch on the terrace of the Régent.

They drove back to the city. Before going to the restaurant, Benjamin wanted to stop at the office to check the mail, which usually included invoices, expert consultations, activity reports, advertisements, and thank-you notes. Benjamin made a quick inventory of the correspondence and noticed a small blue envelope. Jacqueline, who had left for lunch, had unsealed it, which was customary. Benjamin slipped his fingers into the envelope and pulled out a white card. On it, the sender had pasted letters cut out of a magazine. They formed a crude and possibly hastily assembled message:

DO YOU WANT TO NO
ABOUT THE CHATEAU?
GO SEA THE SHEPE
AND YOU WILL UNDERSTAND

"What does that mean?" Virgile asked, looking over his employer's shoulder.

"First of all, it means the fellow who sent this can't spell. Next, he knows us or has spotted us. And finally, he wants to tell us something and has a taste for mystery."

"You're going to enjoy this, aren't you?"

"It is intriguing. And it's the perfect opportunity to drive your Peugeot," Benjamin said, taking the keys right out of Virgile's hand.

"We're not going to eat at the Régent, then?"

"A sandwich will have to do. Unless you prefer some pitted olives."

10

Benjamin drove slowly as they headed out of town. He inhaled the aroma of the leather upholstery, listened to the engine purr, and gauged the responsiveness of the manual transmission. The memory of his grandfather Eugène was so palpable, it wouldn't have surprised him if he had looked in the rearview mirror and seen him sitting in the backseat, his nose sticking out the open window, his mustache in the breeze. The scenery rolled past, and warm air and sun streamed in through the open sunroof.

"This is happiness, Virgile! But don't forget your maintenance. I think the springs need a bit of grease."

"I'll have Stofa take care of it when we pick up your convertible. By the way, you could ask him to service your own car. I think it's been awhile."

"Excellent idea, my boy. I trust you'll make that happen."

"He'll do a good job, as always."

Benjamin tapped the horn lightly as he drove by a cyclist.

"You still haven't told me exactly what we'll be doing in the Médoc, boss."

"Someone sent us an invitation to go see the sheep. So that's where we're headed."

"Sheep at the Château Gayraud-Valrose. Excuse me, but that sounds like a joke. Apart from the Pauillac lamb that often ends up on your plate, I have never seen anything resembling a sheep in the Margaux appellation."

"Of course not, Virgile. But whether this is a prank or a ploy, we have to see what the message means. Someone is giving us a lead. We need to check it out."

Virgile remained quiet, his elbow and forearm resting on the open window, his eyes looking into the distance.

"What's on your mind?" Benjamin asked as he negotiated a curve in the road.

"I've never really understood this appellation, boss. When you hear the name—Margaux—you think of feminine wines, supple and silky. And yet I've tasted all sorts. Some were too diluted, rather dull. Others were more robust and solid. And then there's the terroir, which isn't all that easy to identify on a map. Margaux has always seemed rather complicated."

"You're telling me," Benjamin said, looking over at him. "Defining Margaux in a few words is a real challenge."

Virgile shot his boss a nervous smile. At the mention of Margaux, he had unintentionally strayed onto slippery ground, the name lending itself to allusions and double meanings.

But Benjamin had overcome his morning grouchiness and was feeling much more generous. He eased his assistant's discomfort by summarizing the history of the appellation, which was spread over five townships: Margaux, Cantenac, Soussans, Labarde, and Arsac. He left out none of the well-known struggles and battles those townships had fought to be included in the Margaux appellation. The regulating body, the INAO, hadn't delimited the area geographically until 1954, based on the geological homogeneity of the terroir. This appellation now extended over thirty-five hundred acres of gravelly slopes streaked with clay and sand. It reached as far as the shores of the estuary.

The central diamond of the appellation was the prestigious Château Margaux. Set around it were more or less sizable jewels, some of which had attained brilliant reputations over the years. Benjamin reeled off the names of several grand crus, most of which belonged to the famed 1855 classification established on the recommendation of Napoleon III: Cantenac-Brown,

Brane-Cantenac, Boyd-Cantenac, Pouget, Issan, Kirwan, Desmirail, Prieuré-Lichine, Dauzac, Giscours, Durfort-Vivens, Ferrière, Lascombes, Malescot-Saint-Exupéry, Marquis de Terme, Palmer, Rauzan-Gassies, Rauzan-Ségla, du Tertre, Marquis d'Alesme-Becker, and more.

"Enough already, boss," Virgile said. "The cup is full!"

"Am I overwhelming you, boy? Despite a period of post-war decline, all Margaux wines are worthy, and I count some of them among the most delicate in the Médoc. But one would be wrong to expect them to be silky, supple, round, or lacy simply because of the appellation's feminine name."

"It's true that it's the only terroir with a woman's name," Virgile said quietly, avoiding eye contact with his employer.

"Certainly, the name Margaux connotes a certain nobility and has something of a regal aura. But in the sixteenth century, the word 'Margot' was used to describe a drunk, a girl who couldn't hold her wine. I believe they still use the expression 'you've got a margot' in Lyon when you've tied one on."

Arriving in Cantenac, Benjamin parked under the shade of a billboard in a small square. They left the Peugeot without bothering to lock it and walked toward the town hall.

"What's the plan?" Virgile asked.

"I think we're supposed to look for sheep, right?"

"Yes, indeed. And you think you're going to find them at the town hall?"

"Not really. We are going to consult the land registry."

A secretary led them to the registry without asking any questions. She knew the winemaker, as he had come to the office on several occasions to identify boundaries when land was being partitioned or old vineyards were being consolidated.

"Take all the time you need, Mr. Cooker."

"We won't be long, miss. Thank you."

Benjamin put on his reading glasses and meticulously examined the maps. The Gayraud-Valrose estate extended over some 175 acres, and more than 110 of them were vineyard. The maps contained a wealth of details, including the layout of the plantings, the château, the outbuildings, one well, two springs, and forested areas. At the end of a short trail along the river, there was a rectangular building near a woods. Benjamin put his finger on the map and turned to Virgile.

"Here it is—the sheepfold. We just have to find the sheep."

11

They hid the Peugeot behind a mulberry hedge and slipped down a narrow path lined with weeds and yellowed nettles. A deafening concert of crickets drowned out the cries of seagulls soaring slowly above the river. Making sure that no one was watching, they jumped over a low wall and climbed up the slope where the last vines of the Gayraud-Valrose were standing.

"It never ceases to amaze me," Virgile said quietly. "It's just a miracle to see all these grapes growing in the middle of the scree. Who would believe it?"

"I must say that this soil is among the poorest for grapevines. Very little loam and an abundance of gravel. But look at all these beautiful stones! Centuries and centuries of Garonne floods that have carted, rolled, and polished rocks torn from the Pyrenees. Some of them are magnificent."

Squatting among the vines, they picked up and inspected the sun-warmed stones. Hyaline quartz—blond, purple, and occasionally white if no metallic oxide had tinted them—Jurassic chert, green sandstone, pink and light gray quartzite, shimmering agate, and golden and anthracite flint.

Benjamin watched Virgile's excitement grow as he looked for the most enticing specimens. He gathered them one by one, plunging his hands with delight into the precious piles of stones that smelled of the earth. He filled the pockets of his trousers with the finest examples. Benjamin explained that artisans had once fashioned costume jewelry out of these volcanic and sedimentary stones. In fact, the rocks of the Médoc rivaled those of Bristol, Cayenne, Alençon, and the Rhine.

Virgile listened attentively while continuing his treasure hunt.

"They say that under the reign of King Louis XVI—I think it was shortly before the storming of the Bastille—Count Hargicourt, who was lord of Margaux at the time, made a big impression at Versailles. He arrived wearing a powered wig, silk stockings, beribboned shoes, and a lace jabot. His coat was adorned with dozens of buttons that sparkled like diamonds. People marveled as he passed by. Women whispered. The petty nobles were envious, and finally this sparkling coat came to the king's attention. Imagine the scene: the corpulent Louis XVI approached the count, looked him up and down—from his feet to the last hair on his wig—and before all his courtiers, said, 'Sir, you look like the wealthiest man in the kingdom!' Imagine Hargicourt's embarrassment. He must have been red in the face. But then, with great wit, he gave the monarch a simple and provincial response. He looked at his king with humility and said, 'Sire, I am merely wearing the diamonds of my land.'"

"That's a great story, boss."

"Legend has it that other aristocrats asked local children to gather diamond-like rocks for them. It seems they paid a high price for the times. I don't know if this story is true, but it's fun."

They whispered as they remained crouched in the foliage and tried to go undetected. But this plot at the edge of the property was deserted. No workers. No sounds of agricultural equipment. The way seemed clear, so they carefully stood up and searched the horizon, which was quivering in the heat. Behind a copse of trees, a stone building with a crumbling roof was hidden under ivy and other growth. Benjamin and Virgile approached cautiously, still wary of being spotted.

The door of the abandoned sheepfold was hanging by one rusty hinge. Benjamin and Virgile stepped through a curtain of nervous little flies and entered the building. A pestilential odor immediately assailed them. The heat was dreadful, intensified by the sheet metal workers had used in failed attempts to maintain the roof. The winemaker and his assistant took a few blind steps, squinting and slowly adjusting to the darkness. Around them they made out the shapes of dishes on wooden crates, piles of dirty clothes on the ground, and makeshift beds of burlap bags.

"What is this shit?" Virgile whispered.

"It looks like it's inhabited," Benjamin answered, pointing to two aluminum bowls where blowflies were fighting over a piece of fat stuck in a reddish sauce.

Benjamin pointed to a candle fixed on an empty can near a straw mattress covered with several tattered blankets. Virgile lit it. The soft glow revealed the desolation of the place and the poverty in which the inhabitants of the sheepfold were languishing. Benjamin dug through a big box crammed with packages of macaroni, coarse semolina, and rice. Then he opened an old sports bag with makeshift string handles—the originals were broken. Inside the bag he found six passports stamped with the Moroccan coat of arms. He quickly leafed through them, finding photos of relatively young men, most with moustaches. Some looked world-weary. Others looked more debonair.

"Moroccans?" Virgile asked.

"So it seems. Illegals, no doubt."

"That's no reason to pen them up like dogs! And it stinks in here. The smell's unbearable."

"I wonder where it's coming from," Benjamin said.

"There's no running water in this shack. Look over there. They have buckets filled with water. They must fill them at a spring. I don't think there's a toilet, either."

A muffled moan reached them from the back of the room. Virgile lifted the candle. A shapeless mass was lying on a filthy mattress. They walked over slowly and made out the bald head of a man curled in a fetal position. He had vomited on his blanket and was shaking with fever. His teeth were chattering. He stared at them with terrified dark eyes. Benjamin and Virgile spoke some reassuring words, which the man obviously didn't understand. His cracked and swollen lips were bleeding, but he found the strength to utter a few words in Arabic.

"He must be burning up with fever, and in this heat, I'm amazed he's still alive," Benjamin said.

Virgile was fumbling with his cell phone.

"No bars."

Benjamin looked at the man again and told him he would get help. Benjamin's voice seemed to calm him.

"This is an outrage," Benjamin said.

"Yes, it's absolutely disgusting."

"My first choice of words would probably have been revolting or abject, but I'm with you on this. It is absolutely disgusting. This man needs help right away. We must get to a place with cell coverage and call an ambulance. I'll ring Inspector

97

Barbaroux too. He'll do something about this. And I'm betting it will shed new light on the Rinetti investigation."

Before they left, Virgile filled a plastic bottle with the warm water from the pail near the door and set it down next to the mattress so the man could at least moisten his chapped and swollen lips. They gingerly pulled off the soiled blanket and covered him with a blanket from another mattress that looked cleaner.

"I'm just sorry we can't take him with us and drive him straight to the hospital," Virgile said.

"No, we don't know what he has. It's better that we leave this to the paramedics. We can't do anything more here. Let's go."

12

Benjamin put down the teapot and unfolded the newspaper. The news story took up practically all of the front page. Running across the top was the headline, "An Unsavory Harvest in the Vineyards of Médoc." A photo taken with a telephoto lens captured the crumbling sheepfold between clumps of trees. The foreground, a bit out of focus, showed rows of vines in saturated colors verging on turquoise. In a concise style devoid of metaphor and baroque turns of phrase, the *Sud-Ouest* reporter gave a brief history of the Château Gayraud-Valrose without elaborating on the financial ups and downs of the last heir. The reporter devoted more of the story to the insurance company's buyout and the arrival of the new manager. Some figures on the yield and growth percentages rounded out the exposé.

In a story under a smaller headline, the reporter covered the death of Antoine Rinetti. Having been put in an induced coma after his automobile accident, the young château manager had finally succumbed shortly before midnight. His body would be returned to Nice in the coming days. Funeral arrangements were still being planned.

On a jump page, Benjamin found a story about the unsolved sabotage of Rinetti's Porsche. Margaux was named as a passenger who had also sustained injuries. The reporter didn't mention any leads in the investigation. He enumerated the changes at the estate implemented under Rinetti, but most of the story was speculation. Who had sabotaged Rinetti's car? Why? Did Rinetti have any shadowy connections? Georges Moncaillou's suicide wasn't even brought up.

A companion story was more biting and direct. Several illegal immigrants from Maghreb had been found in an old barn on the estate, according to Inspector Barbaroux. They had been living in deplorable conditions, without even running water. One of them had fallen seriously ill and had been taken to the hospital. The conditions were nothing less than inhumane. Barbaroux recalled a similar situation a few years earlier in a Gironde vineyard.

The winemaker set the newspaper down on the table and drank his cup of Grand Yunnan tea. Without question, the *Sud-Ouest* would follow the story, providing more information as the days wore on. Benjamin pictured the scene at the sheepfold after his departure: the thunderous arrival of police cars, the ambulance whisking the sick man away to the emergency room, the meticulous search of the building, the passport inspection and phone calls to the Moroccan consulate, the fearful faces of the illegal laborers, the district attorney alerted, the prefecture in a frantic state, the search at the château office, the interrogation of the personnel, and Barbaroux's look of delight.

When Benjamin had called the inspector, he hadn't said anything about the anonymous note. The winemaker had merely told him that he was inspecting some vines on the slope near the sheepfold and had ducked into the building because he was curious. Barbaroux seemed to accept the explanation.

"Will you finally be able to enjoy a little more time by the sea, Benjamin?" the inspector had asked. "Your wife and daughter have been spending most of their days there without you."

Elisabeth emerged on the terrace in a light dressing gown, barefoot, wet hair, enveloped in gardenia perfume. She kissed his neck and sat down beside him. Benjamin poured her a cup of tea and began to butter a slice of warm bread for her.

"Orange or apricot?"

"It doesn't matter. I just want you to stop working for a while. You've been under too much stress, and you need a break."

"Aside from the heat, I can assure you that I'm perfectly fine, my sweet."

"You've been preoccupied with your work and worried about Margaux, " Elisabeth answered. "I know it's affected you more than you want to admit."

"Nonsense. She's getting better every day. I can see it."

"Yes, she is recovering, and I'm thankful for that. But she's depressed, Benjamin, and she's still having nightmares about the accident. You're never here, and you don't know what goes on. She tries to act cheerful when she's around you."

"Maybe she is feeling some melancholy. I'm sure she's fatigued from the trauma. But she'll soon be her old self. I'm confident."

"Don't try to minimize this, Benjamin. I'm telling you she's down in the dumps. It's obvious. The only time I've seen her genuinely happy was when she was with Virgile."

"What are you saying?" Benjamin asked, dropping the jelly spoon on the tablecloth. He could feel his blood pressure rising again. "You don't think she's interested in him, do you?"

"I'm not implying anything. I just have the feeling they get along rather well. That's all. And yesterday morning was the first time I've heard Margaux laugh since the accident. It would be good if he stopped by to see her from time to time."

As protective as Elisabeth was, Benjamin didn't think she'd understand his concerns. He just wanted his daughter to find the right man, a man who was capable of settling down and providing for a family. That wasn't Virgile, at least not up to this point.

"We have a lot of work to do at the moment," he told Elisabeth. "And don't forget, wine is his area of expertise. He's no therapist."

"You wouldn't be jealous, by any chance?" Elisabeth asked.

Benjamin looked for a smile on her face, but there was none.

"Me? Jealous? Not at all. I just want the best for the two most important women in my life."

13

Benjamin took a forest-road shortcut from the Truc Vert beach, avoiding the traffic jams in L'Herbe, Canon, and Grand Piquey. At the height of vacation season, getting in and out of the peninsula was difficult. The drive to Bordeaux, which normally took less than an hour, could go on forever, given the endless stream of tourists. Benjamin knew when the flow of cars was light and how to navigate around the current when it was heavy. He had put down the roof of his perfectly serviced Mercedes 280 SL, and it was purring smoothly. Now he could relax and take a deep breath of the invigorating fragrances of pine and fresh sea air, which helped make the morning's high temperature tolerable.

The evening before, he had picked up his convertible at Stofa's garage and fallen into a rather pleasant trap: Ricard, peanuts, and the company of several neighborhood residents. He had been more sensible this time, and the anise-flavored interlude had helped him forget the calamity of the sheepfold, at least temporarily.

Benjamin had also yielded to Elisabeth. He had agreed to bring Virgile to dinner, with the aim of cheering up Margaux. Elisabeth had promised a festive meal: stuffed squid, sea bass grilled in fennel, pureed baby vegetables, and lemon meringue pie. She wanted their stay in Cap Ferret to start feeling like a real vacation.

Once he had reached Bordeaux, the drive to Allées de Tourny was easy, barely disrupted by a slowdown in the commercial section of Mérignac. His assistant was waiting for him in the office. Benjamin found him sitting on the arm of a chair and engaged in a lively discussion with Jacqueline. The topic: washing clothes. Virgile was stressing the importance of doing colorfast cottons in 104-degree water and using an oxygen cleaner. He even knew where to get the best price. Jacqueline, however, was adamant about using another type of detergent.

Benjamin greeted them briefly and went directly to the back room, where the archives were kept.

"Virgile, when you're finished with your dirty laundry, do come and join me, will you?"

The young man complied immediately. They retrieved all the files for the firm's Médoc clients and took them to Benjamin's office to schedule their fieldwork for the coming days.

"If I understand correctly, sir, first we hit the vineyards on the left bank, instead of the right bank, and then we take on the areas of Blaye, Bourg, Castillon, and Saint-Émilion."

"Let's just say that's my plan," Benjamin grumbled. "I know you don't like to have your routine disturbed, but sometimes it's good to shake things up."

"I suppose we'll begin with Margaux, right? And not too far from Château Gayraud-Valrose?"

"I don't need to draw you a map, Virgile. You know very well that I'm curious."

"I also know that even if we work at it as hard as field laborers, we'll never manage to cover the whole territory and see the extent of the damage."

"We're aware that many of the vines are stressed. But this heat wave isn't necessarily a catastrophe. It might even bring about some interesting concentrations. I think you'll be surprised by the quality of the juice they give. But it might not be easy to turn into wine, and we'll need to be careful at the beginning of the fermentation. For now, our job is assessing the vines and, if we can, estimating a date for the harvest."

"I won't be surprised if they start picking before the end of August."

"The way things are going, you wouldn't be wrong. I can't remember any harvest that was earlier. Maybe 1976, but even then, the heat wave wasn't as bad as the one we're having now."

They continued their conversation in the car. Benjamin drove sensibly, looking like a stylish mafioso in a Panama hat. Virgile had doffed a baseball cap. It bore the title of a dark comedy that he enjoyed watching on TV: *Serial Lover*. After they passed through Cantenac, they turned right and took the narrow road leading to Château Gayraud-Valrose.

"As far as I know, this estate is not one of our clients yet," Virgile said.

"Not yet, my boy, but we need to pay our respects. I read in the paper that a condolence notebook was open in the estate office."

Virgile nodded and grinned at Benjamin. The winemaker was pleased that his assistant was beginning to catch on. He had altered the schedule because he didn't want to miss this rare opportunity to penetrate the walls of Gayraud-Valrose.

Benjamin parked in the exact spot he had chosen on their first visit. The gardens were deserted, filled only with the oppressive chirping of cicadas.

They walked by the wine cellar without taking the time to stop and say hello to Stéphane Sarrazin, who was surely working there, enveloped in darkness and silence. The reception desk was at the end of the building. A secretary in an elegant bun greeted them. Benjamin asked to see the steward, and she pushed a button on the intercom to announce their visit. Philippe Cazevielle appeared immediately, crossing the room at a trot.

There was something ridiculous about this short-legged man and his narrow chest, round head, and darting eyes. He looked like a squirrel with cheeks filled with nuts. His rigid posture, defiant chin, and abrupt movements, however, suggested an authoritarian will and a greedy desire to be respected.

"Mr. Cooker? You, here?"

"Delighted, Mr. Cazevielle. Let me introduce my assistant, Virgile Lanssien. We were on our way to Saint-Julien, and we wanted to pay our respects."

"I thank you, sir. The château staff will be very touched by your thoughtfulness."

The conversation began politely, with a certain hypocrisy that Benjamin rather enjoyed. There was no point in coming on too strong. The steward said the estate had suffered a terrible tragedy, and everyone was affected. But Gayraud-Valrose would survive, just as it had since its inception. He just regretted that he wouldn't be able to get away for his superior's funeral service in Nice.

Cazevielle pointed to a large leather-bound book on a nearby table and asked the winemaker to write something. Benjamin ceremoniously uncapped the pen and leaned over the white page offered to him. On previous pages, neighboring property owners had expressed their own condolences. Benjamin skimmed them before putting down his thoughts. He cleared his throat and began writing. "May the future vintages of Château Gayraud-Valrose comfort us in our grief, sustain our memory, open our minds, and lift our spirits." He signed with a flourish: the name Benjamin Cooker extended, round and proud, across the page like billowing sails in a threatening storm.

Casually returning the pen to its place on the table, Benjamin turned to Cazevielle. It was time to get down to business. "But what about this awful situation with the Moroccan workers?" he asked.

Philippe Cazevielle blanched, tensed, and straightened up, as if to look taller before the winemaker's imposing figure.

"Newspapers always exaggerate things," he said.

"Of course, but I'm given to understand that the police are investigating, and most certainly, French labor laws have been violated. As the steward, you are legally in charge of the estate at the present time."

"As I said, we've been preoccupied with Antoine Rinetti's death. The police investigators took my statement, and they completely understand that I had nothing to do with the hiring and living conditions of those men."

"So you knew these men were working in your vineyards."

"Nothing gets past me, sir. I've been working here for seventeen years, and there is not an acre that I don't know. Not a single employee is foreign to me."

"Indeed, let's talk about the foreigners. These illegal Moroccans had been on your estate for more than three months."

"They came here right after Antoine Rinetti's appointment, and I never hid my disapproval from him. He had cut the payroll and let some of our regular workers go. Shortly after that, we saw these poor fellows arrive, and he put them in the old sheepfold."

"You must have known that they had no visas or work permits. They were undocumented."

"I told you. Nothing escapes me."

"I heard you, Mr. Cazevielle. And you also knew that their living conditions were nothing less than reprehensible."

The steward sighed and lowered his head. He was losing his haughty air and feigned confidence.

"I had several heated discussions with Mr. Rinetti. I told him explicitly that the way he was treating those men was offensive and immoral. I said he had to do something about it."

"When you say 'heated discussions,' what do you mean?"

"Very heated. It came to blows."

"Is that so!"

"Yes. It happened only once, and we hardly spoke after that. I knew I was in the hot seat—everyone was—and he would eventually get rid of me, like he did the others."

"You mean Georges Moncaillou, I guess?"

"I was sick over that. The old man had been here for more than thirty years, and we owed him a lot."

"Mr. Cazevielle, just how angry were you with Mr. Rinetti? Enough to sabotage his car?"

"Mr. Cooker! How could you even suggest that? All we did was argue."

"You should have done more than argue with your employer, Mr. Cazevielle. In the eyes of the law, you are an accomplice to the exploitation of those migrant workers."

"I was afraid of causing a scandal that would compromise the reputation of the château. I thought the Moroccans would be here for only a short time, that they would leave after the harvest, but…"

There was a long silence. His arms crossed and his feet planted firmly on the floor, Benjamin towered over the steward, who seemed to be shrinking as the conversation continued.

"But?" Benjamin repeated.

"I think things wouldn't have changed, even with time. Quite the contrary."

There was no point in continuing. The conversation had been edifying enough, and it would serve no purpose to intimidate any further this man trapped in his own contradictions, resignation, and remorse. Benjamin extended his hand in parting, and when Virgile approached to do the same, the steward looked shocked.

"Young man, I didn't make the connection when Mr. Cooker introduced you, but this isn't the first time we've met."

"No, it's not. I did an internship here."

"I remember now. Your hair was longer at the time."

"That's true, Mr. Cazevielle. You're right. Nothing escapes you."

14

Benjamin ordered a tomato and mozzarella salad and melon with Serrano ham, along with a bottle of mineral water in an ice bucket. His dining companion was wavering between pan-fried calf's liver and veal sweetbreads in ravigote sauce. Benjamin wondered how anyone could have an appetite in such hot weather. He watched as Inspector Barbaroux weighed yet another decision: a 1999 Léoville Poyferré or a 1996 Léoville Las Cases?

"Well, I'll have a Pauillac... A Pontet-Canet... You only have a 1998? Okay, that will do. What do you think, Mr. Cooker?"

"I think very little in this heat. I feel like my brains are *fromage blanc*."

"Oh, that's funny. You have such an English sense of humor."

"No, actually, it's something that my assistant said this morning when we were in the vineyards."

"That young man seems very nice. He has a thoughtful look about him, and he's charming, too, which doesn't hurt. He exudes a certain joie de vivre."

"You're not the only one who thinks that," Benjamin muttered.

The inspector had called Benjamin earlier in the day. The man was typically blunt and too the point. He had always been full of convoluted sentences and pointless questions. The winemaker thought it wise to invite him to lunch at Noailles. It would give them the opportunity to update each other on their respective investigations.

"So, what's going on with your colleagues in Nice?"

"No news. I'm still waiting. Their investigators are probably rummaging through garbage cans and searching desks for hidden compartments. Those boys love to wallow in dirty little secrets."

"I suppose the discovery of the Moroccan workers has given your investigation a boost."

"Thanks again for tipping us off. It wasn't hard to find those men. They were slaving away on a parcel near the secondary road: five guys breaking their backs for twenty euros a day. As far as the sheepfold goes, our people searched everything, and it was vile. But I don't need to tell you that. You saw it yourself. The guy they took to the hospital is improving, according to the doctors. Fortunately, he didn't have anything contagious, but he was in a bad way, completely dehydrated and malnourished—getting bedsores, too. I'll spare you the details. I don't want to ruin your appetite."

"I can't understand how anyone could treat people that way," Benjamin sighed. "Man's disregard for human life frightens me, and I always…"

"But you weren't born yesterday," Barbaroux interrupted. There was a note of cynicism in his tone. "You know as well as I do that people can do horrendous things, commit despicable acts of cruelty. Or are you're pretending to be above all that?"

"No, I'll just never get used to it."

Benjamin drank some water to loosen his throat and calm himself. He was feeling both angry and disgusted.

"There's a question that's been bugging me," the inspector continued, sniffing his glass of Pontet-Canet. "How did you happen to find yourself in that barn? I don't believe you had any reason to be on the estate."

"I've been waiting for you to ask that question."

From the inside pocket of his jacket, he took out the little blue envelope containing the anonymous letter. Barbaroux reached for it and read the text.

"The entire execution is crude. The letters are from *Sud-Ouest* clippings, without a doubt. It looks like a bad poison-pen letter. Maybe the person who sent this is a fan of police shows on TV. In any case, the author isn't necessarily uneducated or ignorant, but the spelling suggests that he or she could have dyslexia or some other problem with comprehension. I've known a couple of people like this who managed to get through school but always had issues with reading and spelling. It really made learning difficult. I'm going to send the letter to the lab for fingerprints. You never know."

"You will definitely find my fingerprints and Jacqueline's. She's my secretary."

"We know how to do our job, Mr. Cooker. No worries."

The waiter brought the calf's liver with house-made fries. Barbaroux licked his chops and tucked his napkin under his chin like a country boy. Benjamin was surprised—almost shocked. He delicately cut his slice of melon and waited until the inspector had swallowed his first bite before continuing.

"I have no idea who could have sent me such a note."

"In that case, you have to ask yourself four questions. First: who mailed the letter? Second: why? Third: why to you? And finally: what were the sender's intentions?"

"You make it sound entirely cut-and-dried."

"Oh, don't misunderstand. Investigating isn't an exact science. Sure, we have labs full of equipment and computer search engines at our fingertips. Our forensic capabilities make taxpayers feel like their money's well spent. But in the end, nothing's as good as the sixth sense and intuition.

You follow your nose and keep your eyes open. I imagine it's kind of the same thing in your work."

"In some ways."

The inspector was chewing loudly and talking with his mouth open. He methodically took a big gulp of Pauillac with every two bites of meat. He was sweating profusely and used his cloth napkin to wipe his face.

"In my opinion, we don't have to search very far," Barbaroux continued, bringing a forkful of fries to his mouth. "The person who sent this note is someone who works on the estate and didn't like what was going on. Maybe this person wanted to get rid of the illegals. After all, they were taking bread out of the mouths of Médoc workers. Maybe the sender thought you would have the most clout. He or she wanted to implicate the château management, perhaps the steward and certainly the insurance company that owns the place and puts itself above the law."

"That's one possible explanation, among others," Benjamin said, shrugging.

"Why? Do you have another theory?"

"I'm thinking along similar lines. But I'm also wondering if the Moroccans and the anonymous letter are connected to the sabotage of the Porsche."

"You'd make a good cop, Mr. Cooker. We must answer that question. Maybe the person who sent the letter was also the one who sabotaged the

Porsche. But the author of the note could have sent it long ago and gotten the same result without feeling any need to tamper with Rinetti's car."

"That's very true, but Antoine Rinetti might have been the victim of someone who wanted to make him pay for his actions, especially hiring illegals."

Using his last fries, the inspector wiped his plate clean. Every spot of sauce was gone. The methodical gesture bothered Benjamin, who took it as an attempt to end the discussion.

"What are your thoughts?" the winemaker asked sharply, unable to conceal his annoyance.

"I think you're an honest guy."

"You've known that for some time, Inspector Barbaroux."

"I know, but that's never enough for me. I need to be reassured."

"What are you trying to say?"

"What did the steward tell you this morning?"

"How did you find out that I was at Gayraud-Valrose? Of course I've made no secret of it, but I'd like to know who informed you. If you go on like that, I'll get the impression that you have someone following me."

"I have my sources. Let's just say that I'm getting regular reports on traffic in and out of that château. It's my job. You're not going to hold that against me, are you?"

Benjamin nodded and summarized his meeting with Philippe Cazevielle without omitting any of his personal impressions.

"That jibes with the interrogation we put him through. He's a complicated dude who made the mistake of turning a blind eye. Now he's implicated in our criminal investigation, and after the funeral we will definitely get a request from the prosecutor to arrest him for labor-law violations."

"Will he face a heavy sentence if he's found guilty?"

"At the least he'll be charged with complicity, and that is pretty serious."

"Do you think he could have sabotaged the car to get rid of Rinetti? They had come to blows and hadn't been on speaking terms for quite a while."

"I don't think so. He wouldn't have had the means."

"What means?"

"I mean the ability."

"Be clearer. You usually say too much, but now you're not saying enough. Please get to the point."

"Shit, I might as well tell you. We have new information that leads me to believe that Cazevielle didn't sabotage the car. You have to promise that you'll keep this to yourself. Besides me and my close colleagues, you'll be the only one to know."

"You do me great honor, Inspector," the winemaker muttered, forcing himself to sound polite.

"Spare me your sarcasm, Mr. Cooker. I got a phone call from our forensics team last night. They wanted to talk with me in person. I went to the garage, and they were standing around the Porsche, waiting for me. With the evidence charred, the chassis twisted, and the parts blackened, finding clues had been hard. But finally one of them noticed something abnormal about the steering. A connection from the pump to the rotary valve was loose."

"You mean someone also tried to sabotage the power steering?"

"Forensics is sure of it. It couldn't have come loose in the accident. You need the right tool and a good strong turn for that to happen."

"Rinetti didn't stand a chance," Benjamin said.

"And your daughter escaped all the more miraculously. Rinetti had absolutely no control of the car."

"But why are you so sure the steward didn't sabotage the car?"

"Because you have to know how to work on a car, and we checked, the steward is hardly a mechanic. The person who did this had to be an expert, and he had to act quickly. The car was parked in an outbuilding very close to the château. People were in and out of that building all the time. He had to lift the car with a jack, put a wedge under a tire to keep it from moving, and then slide under the chassis to carry out his dirty work before doing it all over again in reverse: lower the car, take the jack out, and remove the wedge. And he had to get out of that building without being seen. I haven't even mentioned the clippers he used to cut the brake-fluid hose."

"Clippers?"

"Yes, we found a pair with the Bahco insignia on the blade. Evidently, it's not a harvesting pruner, but rather a big pair of shears used for cutting the vines. There's no doubt about that, either."

"But I'm still not entirely convinced that Cazevielle's in the clear."

"As I said, the man's clueless when it comes to mechanics. We went through his car's service record with a fine-tooth comb and talked to his mechanic. Cazevielle wouldn't be able to find his dipstick if a gun were pressed to his head, believe me. What's more, he has an elbow problem, a tennis elbow that gives him chronic pain. He has trouble loosening an ordinary screw."

Benjamin said nothing. He had too many questions. Barbaroux's inside information only muddled things.

"I don't think this wine is all that great," the inspector said, polishing off the glass.

"You haven't had any trouble getting it down, though. What's wrong with it?"

Benjamin emptied his glass of mineral water in one swallow and poured himself a mouthful of

Pauillac. He took a sip, rolled the wine under his tongue and spit it into the glass.

"It's a bit corked. Not all that much, but still…"

"Oh, okay, that's why. That slight taste of dirty cassock. I thought it smelled like an old priest."

Benjamin couldn't help laughing. He called the waiter to explain that the bottle was defective. Looking profoundly embarrassed, the waiter hurried away and promptly returned with another bottle.

"And since we're talking shop, what do you think of those screw tops we're seeing on more bottles these days? Do you think corks are on the way out?"

"I always try not to have an opinion, only doubts."

"A doubt is an opinion of sorts," the inspector said. He sounded a bit sly.

The winemaker considered Barbaroux's comment a moment and then said, "According to studies, two to three percent of the nearly eight hundred million bottles produced in Bordeaux each year have cork taint. That's a chemical compound created when natural fungi in the cork came in contact with chlorides and other substances found in a winery's sterilization products. The percentage seems insignificant, but it translates to some eighteen million bottles that can't be drunk because they smell and taste soggy and rotten."

"So is that an argument for screw tops, Mr. Cooker?"

"Some French vintners are following the lead of vineyards in Australia, New Zealand, and Chili, and have adopted an aluminum cap with a gas-tight seal. It does solve the problem of cork taint, my good man, but still, that is no way to store wine. Nothing could ever replace the cork, with its flexibility and ability to breathe and enhance aging."

"Well, how then do you get rid of cork taint?"

"I don't think it could be entirely eradicated, but insisting on quality corks would go a long way toward minimizing the problem. Wine is a living thing," he concluded with conviction. "We'll be lost if we forget that!"

"That may be true," Barbaroux said. "But to claim, as some do, that wine has a soul—that's going too far!"

"Of course wine has a soul!" Benjamin said, raising his voice. He could feel his cheeks getting red. "You need to read Baudelaire." He cleared his throat.

> "One eve in the bottle sang the soul of wine:
> 'Man, unto thee, dear disinherited,
> I sing a song of love and light divine—
> Prisoned in glass beneath my seals of red.'"

"I'm not one for poetry, Mr. Cooker."

"Wine has both a life and a soul. Without a cork, the angels cannot take their share. And where you exclude the angels, you exclude God and His miracles. What fools would commit such sacrilege?"

"I'm not really following you."

"Those who would try to force perfection—by using an aluminum cap, for example—are bound to fail. You see, perfection is an illusion. It's never attainable. Miracles, on the other hand, happen all the time. And they often masquerade as mistakes. Take Sauterne. It's an accumulation of coincidences, approximations, trial and error. It's the most beautiful mistake there ever was!"

"That's true," Barbaroux admitted. "By the way, I enjoyed the section on sweet wines in your guide."

"Vanity is also a factor in this whole issue of perfection. I've seen people put a bottle on the table as though they were dropping their pants and showing off their cocks. You know—bigger is always better. Excellent vintage, prestigious label, exorbitant price. It makes you important and gives you power. At least it affirms your social status."

"Wow, how you can go on! Showing off their cocks—seriously?"

"Yes, except even the most extravagant and perfect-looking wine can be flawed."

"That's a possibility, I suppose."

"It's the same thing when you find yourself in bed with a woman for the first time. She looks sublime. You undress her, and then, when you see her without her clothes on, her breasts aren't the way you imagined them. Her stomach isn't as firm as you thought, or maybe her scent and skin don't excite you. I'm sure women have a similar reaction when they wind up in bed with a man whose paunch is too big or whose balls are too hairy."

"Cork taint."

"Absolutely. You're following me. It's part and parcel of the mystery that we must preserve. You have to risk being let down if you're open to experiencing wine in all its miraculous wonder. I'm a hundred percent for bad surprises, disappointment, exasperation, exaggerated remarks—and why not exorbitant price tags—if it makes you excited about the adventure. And to thoroughly appreciate that adventure, you must allow wine to be itself. As far as I'm concerned, too many producers have just one pragmatic aim: making a profit. They're entirely too willing to keep their wine sealed under plastic, locked under a cap, hopelessly impenetrable if it means making more money."

"I didn't know you were so lyrical. So you're actually a sensitive man and a little bit of a mystic, Mr. Cooker."

The winemaker stuck the tines of his fork into a cherry tomato. The skin burst open, spitting a spot of sanguine pulp onto the edge of his plate. It looked like a splotch of blood created by a movie makeup artist.

"That's because you've never read me carefully, Inspector. You must always look for what's
happening between the lines." After a moment of
silence, he added, "Hmm, that makes me wonder what we are missing at the château. Perhaps,
Inspector, we do need a more careful reading
there too."

15

Margaux spent the better part of her days reading. She had found shelves full of detective novels at the back of a closet at La Planquette, and she devoured dozens of the dog-eared paperbacks with faded covers and yellowed pages. She loved Georges Simenon's plots. The slow pace, odd characters, and provincial rhythm spoke to her more than American hard-boiled fiction with their bursts of gunfire, bloody pursuits, and plot twists on every page. Spy thrillers intrigued her even less. Although they always made the best-seller lists, too many were formulaic, as far as she was concerned.

From time to time she opened a cyanide-laced homicide concocted by old English ladies whose Victorian perversions she adored. Margaux's literary inclinations were those of a young woman who knew she was privileged but loved to escape her era. Far from the noise and bustle of New York, she relished this interlude in the land of her childhood. Stretched out on a blue-and-white deck chair or lying on the living room chaise lounge, she turned the pages to the sound of the cicadas, an iced tea on the table beside her.

When Virgile suggested leaving La Planquette for a change of scenery, Margaux hesitated. She knew the nightlife at Cap Ferret all too well and didn't miss those aimless outings. There were only two places that interested her. One was the Sail Fish, with its inviting décor, efficient staff, and proper menus. The crowd from the end of the peninsula was always there: the affluent and the nouveau riche of western Paris, middle-class young people from Bordeaux, silicone creatures who came to flaunt their navels, and a sprinkle of celebrities. At two in the morning, when the restaurant closed, most of them migrated to the second spot, the New Centaure, a sweltering nightclub where you could lose yourself in the music, despite the smoky air and the sweaty patrons.

Margaux didn't know what Virgile was thinking, anyway. She'd never be able to navigate a disco with her crutches, much less dance. But she didn't want to disappoint him. She agreed to go to Tchanqué, where they could quietly enjoy rum and tapas on the terrace.

Sitting comfortably with their glasses of white Pessac-Léognan, Margaux and Virgile were finally alone for the first time. And Margaux found that she and Virgile had a lot to talk about. They started with casual subjects that allowed each of them to get used to the other's voice, nuances, brief silences, and gestures. They ordered another glass of the same wine, a 2000 Château de France, and then easily recalled personal memories, some of which they had never revealed to anyone else.

Margaux spoke at length of her childhood at Grangebelle: playing hide-and-seek between the barrels, the extravagant dolls from her grandfather in London, her friends from primary school at Saint-Julien-de-Beychevelle, and her aunt, who had predicted her future by reading her palm. She went on to discuss her overly serious studies at business school and her move to New York and an apartment building full of friendly nutcases. She laughed a lot, loudly and happily, when Virgile recalled his youth in the Montravel countryside, bicycles swapped, slingshots fashioned from hazelnut branches, traps jerry-rigged to catch lizards, the Bergerac fairgrounds, the groping hands of the rowing club monitor, his old pal Thomasseau's crib sheet, and the over-the-top fiestas in a Spanish bar near the Place de la Victoire.

Their paths had been noticeably different, and they had come from different social classes. But because both of them had grown up in southwest France, they had much in common. They had been raised among the vines and along the quays of the port of Bordeaux, under the changing skies that reflected the moods of the ocean. Margaux and Virgile talked and talked, making no attempt to seduce each other with flattery or indulge in the ritual of the mating dance. And they lingered too long on the terrace, where the soft light seemed to protect them from the rest of the world.

"Do you see the time?" Margaux said, looking at her watch. "Maman has spent hours making dinner for us. They must be sitting at the table already. She'll be furious!"

"Don't worry, Margaux. I'll get us back there as quickly as I can. I may not drive a Porsche, like Rinetti, but my old Peugeot 403 can hold its own."

"Please, Virgile, don't get the wrong idea. That poor man was very proper. But like some other fellows I've met, he thought he was the center of the universe. He talked about himself a lot, and he wasn't very interested in my life."

As they got into the Peugeot, Virgile apologized for mentioning Rinetti. "I was out of line," he said softly, touching her forearm. He immediately withdrew his hand and started the engine.

Margaux understood. She was the boss's daughter, and her father was even more protective than usual these days, given her brush with death. The last thing Virgile needed was a punch in the nose from her dad.

They arrived just as everyone was getting ready to taste the stuffed squid. They quickly apologized and sat down noisily to distract from the Ludovic's teasing remarks, Elisabeth's affectionate reproaches, Leslie's tender gaze, and Benjamin's tense silence. They marveled over the delicacy of the sauce, the perfect preparation, and the choice of wine, a 1999 premier cru Clos Saint-Jacques from Domaine de la Folie.

"Benjamin gave me a hand in the kitchen, which was much appreciated," Elisabeth said, raising her glass to her husband. "And it's a good thing that we eat late," she added, winking at her daughter. "Virgile, you'll meet Leslie and Ludovic's children tomorrow. Their mom and dad wore them out today, and they couldn't keep their eyes open past eight."

The breeze from the ocean had failed to bring down the temperature more than a few degrees, and the conversation inevitably came around to the heat wave and the news. Hundreds had died, according to the papers. Some experts, including well-known scientists, were saying the weather was yet another indication of climate change and more serious consequences to come.

"I read a particularly ominous prediction," Ludovic ventured. "The Arcachon Bay will become a lake. The Pointe de Grave will be an island. Storms and tornadoes will be the norm. The beaches of Landes will shrink before our eyes. Insects from the tropics will bring malaria. Fish from the Caribbean will appear on our shores. Snow will become rare in the Pyrenees. The rocky coasts of the Basque country will fall to erosion. But palm, mandarin, and olive trees will grow in abundance. I don't know about you, but a few more palm and olive trees aren't enough to make me look forward to any of that."

"And we'd be out of a job, boss, unless everyone around here started making palm wine," Virgile said. "Damn, I can just see you climbing palm trees to check out the fruit."

Everyone turned to Benjamin, but he just sat there, silent, sipping his wine.

When the lemon meringue pie was all gone, a purple bolt of lightning streaked through the sky. Thunder clapped in the port of La Vigne. They had hoped for this storm for so many days, and at last it had arrived. They rushed to clear the table, covered the teakwood furniture, and dashed inside. A deafening roar, a sudden rain, fierce gusts of wind—and then nothing. They all looked outside to see if the storm had done any damage, and seeing nothing, Elisabeth and Benjamin and Ludovic and Leslie decided to go to bed.

Virgile went into the backyard to duck into the Canadian tent Ludovic had pitched for him. Margaux hobbled outside to make sure the ground under the tent was still dry, feeling her father's eyes on them the whole way. Couldn't he just relax a little? She sighed and went back into the house.

16

The first thing Benjamin Cooker did when he got out of bed the next morning was make sure Margaux was sleeping peacefully in her room. He found her dozing soundly, her face buried in the pillow. When he kissed her cheek, she shivered slightly and turned to her other side. His mind at ease, he carefully closed the door and made himself a piping-hot cup of tea. He turned on the coffeemaker for the others.

He had decided to spend the day at La Planquette and do nothing but enjoy his family. There was no point in worrying about all the files left unfinished. The drought continued, and any advice from Cooker & Co. wouldn't change that.

He had nothing to contribute to the Château Gayraud-Valrose investigation either. The contradictory information had thrown him off. It would be better to leave it to the professionalism of Inspector Barbaroux. At this point, Benjamin had no reason to be involved. All he could really do was offer his discreet support to the police, who seemed to be handling matters and proceeding methodically.

Yes, it was far better to take refuge in the sweet comfort of Cap Ferret, although it was unfortunate that the fishing boat had broken down. The engine had definitely given up the ghost. Ludovic had rushed around looking for a repairman, but all the shipyards were up to their necks in work. No one could service the boat for two months. Leslie and Ludovic were disappointed. They had been looking forward to organizing a picnic on the Banc d'Arguin.

Virgile crawled out of his tent shortly after the coffee had finished dripping. Benjamin watched through the window as his assistant stood up, yawned, and rubbed the small of his back before trudging toward the house. The winemaker poured some coffee for his assistant and joined him on the terrace, where he had dropped into a chair. Virgile mumbled a dull hello.

"Sleep well, son?"

"An army of mosquitoes invaded through a hole in the tent, the inflatable mattress went flat, the sleeping bag was too hot, and a couple of noisy raccoons kept me entertained. It was a great night, boss!"

Margaux and Elisabeth soon joined them at the table, bright-eyed and bushy-tailed, their cheeks rosy and smiles on their faces. Ludovic and Leslie Lamotte surfaced with their children,

Victor and Aristide, who had jumped on their bed to awaken them. A tickling session that followed had put the little family in a good mood.

The women decided to go to the market and spend the rest of the day by the water. They opted for the little beach at the port of La Vigne overlooking the bay, which was a few hundred yards from the villa. There was a shady spot where Margaux could rest peacefully, not to mention the ice cream man, a major selling point for the children. Ludovic promised to join them later, after he tried one last time to contact some boating companies in the department of Gironde. Benjamin was a bit vague about his plans. He was behind in his reading and would come by to stick his feet in the water before going to his six o'clock book signing at the Alice Bookstore. Recovered from the effects of his broken sleep, Virgile announced that he would follow the crowd and go swimming, as there was nothing else to do.

The beginning of the day unfolded as planned: the women and children on the sand, Ludovic on his laptop, looking for boat-repair shops, and Benjamin immersed in some very dry oenology reports. Virgile had taken off with the rest of the group, making sure they had all their beach umbrellas, provisions, cooler, magazines, shovels, pails, and rakes. He had promised to help the children build sand castles. Two hours later, however, Benjamin spotted his assistant walking back to La Planquette.

"What? Back already? I thought you were looking forward to spending a day with the ladies, Virgile."

"Sorry, boss. I've had my dose of vacation. That's it!" he said, all smiles as he stepped onto the terrace and pulled out a chair.

Benjamin took off his glasses and put down his magazine.

"So now you know, son. Many successful relationships are based on a fundamental principle. The ladies go out and do their thing, and the men stay behind and putter—although sometimes it's the other way around. Welcome to the club. I suspected that you'd be coming back, but I have to give you credit for lasting longer than I thought you would."

The assistant poured himself a glass of cold lemonade and sat down.

"Sir, I've been thinking about what Barbaroux told you. There may be a way to confirm a few things."

"You're supposed to be relaxing, son. Don't be worrying about that."

"I'm not worried at all. Actually, I think I have a good idea."

"Fire away. The sea air can be good for the brain."

"Seriously, boss. We've been going at this head-on. A sly approach might just help us figure out who sabotaged the car. Are you following my line of thought?"

"Not at all."

"Maybe I could take a drive in the vicinity of Gayraud-Valrose and see to it that my Peugeot breaks down. Then I could ask for help at the château and wait for someone to assist me. I'll flush out that damned mechanic! If he's able to smash up cars, he can fix mine."

"I don't really think your plan will work. And you'll run the risk of making someone suspicious. Need I remind you that we were poking around there recently?"

"I could tell them that I was on my way to another estate. And I assure you, disabling a car isn't that complicated. I called Stofa from the beach, and he explained how to do it. Of course, he wondered why I would do such a thing, and I had to tell him it was a prank. I don't think he believed me, but hey, I'll fill him in later. The idea is simple. I just unscrew the distributor cap, take out the ignition rotor with a flathead screwdriver, and close the breaker points. Not too much, just enough to cause a breakdown that looks real."

"And you want to go there now?"

"Right away. There's no sense in wasting any time. Oh, and Ludovic will be happy to hear this. Tell him Stofa's dropping by this afternoon to take a look at the fishing boat motor."

"Now that's great news!"

"Yes, business is slow at the garage right now, so he's happy to come over and give you guys a hand. I don't know why, but he seems to think you're a nice guy. Just joking, boss."

17

The outline of the château stood out, imposing yet elegant, against a dark-blue sky so intense, it seemed to be painted with the broad strokes of a brush. The countryside was dozing amid murmuring insects. In the distance, workers were bent in the vineyard, removing undesirable shoots, spraying copper sulfate, and cutting the tops of the vine stocks. Between the flowering and the onset of ripening, work on the vines was ceaseless. There was the continual threat of infestation, and couch grass and bindweed had to be pulled up.

Virgile slowed down when he came to the right spot, out of sight, where the drive to the estate met the road. He popped the hood of the Peugeot and followed Stofa's instructions. In case someone was watching, he slid back behind the wheel and tried to start the engine several times. He got out quickly, acted annoyed—swearing louder than necessary—kicked the tire, and headed up the drive to the château. Stéphane Sarrazin gave him a friendly wave when he saw him and walked over to see what was wrong. Sweating and anxious-looking, Virgile told Sarrazin why he was there.

"No need for that long face," Sarrazin said. "It's a good thing you broke down here. Let's see what's going on."

Sarrazin told Virgile to follow him to a nearby spot in the vineyard where Gilles Moncaillou, old Georges's son, was working on supports for the vines. According to the cellar master, Gilles wasn't exceptionally smart and was even a little backward, but he could spend hours tinkering with his moped. He did an adequate job of maintaining the estate's equipment and repairing the farm machinery.

Virgile was surprised when he realized that the younger Moncaillou had no memory of his internship. It hadn't been that long ago, and Virgile and Gilles had gotten along reasonably well under the tutelage of the father, whose swearing was sorely missed among the vines. The vines seemed almost too reined-in these days. Stéphane Sarrazin asked Gilles if he could try his hand at repairing the Peugeot 403 at the end of the drive.

Gilles continued working on the vines and didn't even look at Virgile. Finally he said, "Got any tools in the car?"

Virgile, taken aback, nodded, and Gilles followed them.

It took them a long time to find the problem. With the help of Sarrazin, whose mechanical knowledge was rather limited, Gilles Moncaillou attacked the carburetor and the gas line before looking at the air filter, spark plugs, and battery connections. They carefully and methodically tightened and untightened the nuts, bolts, and screws. Their hands became dark with grease, but they never lost patience. Some of what they did totally escaped Virgile's attention. He was getting parched under the merciless sun. But eventually Gilles and Sarrazin unscrewed the distributor cap, removed the ignition rotor, and took care of the issue. The unremarkable heir of Georges Moncaillou had no particular reaction when Virgile slipped behind the wheel and turned the key, and the Peugeot once again hummed.

"Thank you. You saved me, guys!"

"That car of yours was a pain in the ass," Gilles spit out before returning to his vines.

Stéphane Sarrazin invited Virgile to come and wash off under the tap in the wine cellar. They splashed themselves with cool water, drinking as much as washing, and finished by tasting the château's last vintage, whose tannins were not as poorly extracted as Benjamin Cooker had claimed in his guide.

"You must admit, we've made progress since the last edition of the *Cooker Guide*," said the cellar master. "Here, take a case. Keep half for yourself, and give the rest to your boss. He'll surely change his mind."

18

Benjamin enjoyed meeting his readers. It gave him the opportunity to put faces to at least some of the people who made the effort to consult the more than eight hundred pages of the *Cooker Guide*. And the winemaker was especially fond of this particular bookstore. The Alice Bookstore had the enormous appeal of providing not only a large range of publications, but also a very well-stocked wine cellar. The winemaker was seated in front of the store window, behind a long wooden table. He was in high spirits as he signed his guide, making sure each was personalized and happily answering even the most absurd questions.

The patrons at the bookstore were a reflection of Cap Ferret as a whole: friendly and cultured. Conversations were polite and well informed. Besides the old Bordeaux families who had owned rustic vacation homes with large windows overlooking the water for many generations, Cap Ferret was populated with a chic set who liked to have a sense of belonging. Anyone who worked in fashion, media, advertising, entertainment, wholesale clothing, retail jewelry, public relations, or financial advising in Paris's monied neighborhoods was certain to find at least one colleague from the Trocadéro office, a neighbor from Passy, an antique dealer from Neuilly, a tennis partner from Auteuil, or a competitor from Faubourg Saint-Honoré.

But despite the old and new money and the celebrity of many who spent their summers on the peninsula, Cap Ferret was still a place where families could vacation and where bicycles were often the preferred mode of transportation. Mothers didn't have to worry about their hair and makeup, and the food grilled at backyard barbecues was frequently better than the daily specials at the best restaurants.

There were only a dozen copies of the *Cooker Guide* left on the table when Benjamin said goodbye and left the Alice bookstore. The event had been a clear success, and he promised to return for at least one more signing before the end of the season.

When the winemaker arrived at La Planquette, Virgile was back from his expedition. He was in the living room with Margaux, who was giving him a lesson on painters who had been seduced by the Arcachon light. The walls of the room were filled with reproductions and prints depicting various perspectives of the bay. Virgile seemed taken with a watercolor by Jean-Paul Alaux that evoked the Côte de Piraillan in delicate strokes reflecting a Japanese influence. He lingered before a sunset by Adrien Dauzats, an etching by Léo Drouyn, an oil painting of the forest in La Teste by Louis Augustin Auguin, and a shipwreck by Amédée Baudit. A beautiful interior scene by Édouard Manet seemed to captivate him the most. A figure in dark attire was leaning on a pedestal table, giving an impression of idleness in the delicate light streaming through an open window.

"Papa, did you know that Virgile had such a sharp eye?" Margaux said, kissing her father hello.

"No, but I'm not surprised. To be a wine taster, you must have heightened senses."

"Thank you for the compliment," Virgile said, looking embarrassed.

"You seem surprised, Virgile. Is it that unusual to get a compliment from my father?"

Benjamin wasn't about to let Virgile answer the question. Besides, he wanted to hear how his assistant's trip had gone.

"So tell me, Virgile, what did your little subterfuge turn up?"

"Hit a brick wall, sir. I spent the afternoon with Stéphane Sarrazin and Gilles Moncaillou, and I doubt that either of them has a future in auto repair. Quite honestly, if they were as talented as Barbaroux thinks, they would have found the problem in ten minutes. We'll have to look elsewhere."

"At any rate, it wasn't a waste of time. Two fewer suspects on the list. By the way, your friends Stofa and Salem still haven't come back from the port. It's starting to get dark, and I have the feeling the motor is really done for."

"I know Stofa, and I'd be surprised if he couldn't fix it."

At that very moment, Ludovic came running into the room, pulling his polo shirt over his head like a victorious soccer player, a big grin on his face.

"There, what did I tell you?" Virgile said, beaming at Benjamin.

"Yes, yes, yes! The boat is going full blast! Yes, Virgile, your Bordeaux friends are fantastic!"

Stofa and Salem followed him in, their tool boxes under their arms. Benjamin, Virgile, Ludovic, and Margaux gave the pair a hero's welcome. Then Benjamin showed them to the bathroom, where they could clean up, and invited them to join everyone else on the terrace.

"Gentlemen, I don't know if it's cocktail hour yet, but you've certainly earned a drink," Benjamin said as soon as Stofa and Salem appeared on the terrace. "I'm sorry we don't have a drop of Ricard in the house. But we have a lot of wine. Let me check on our chilled white and rosé."

"Uh-oh. I completely forgot to put them in the fridge this morning," Ludovic said. "I was so pre-occupied with getting the boat motor fixed."

"In that case, we'll make do with red. I hope you gentlemen don't mind."

"Red it is," Stofa said, plunging his hand into a ramequin filled with peanuts.

"What would you say to a Gayraud-Valrose? Our dear Virgile brought us some today."

"What's that you said?" Stofa asked. "A Gayraud-Valrose?"

"Yes, a Gayraud-Valrose. Would you prefer something else?"

"Oh, no! I don't know much about wine, but that one's a standout. An old friend of mine has been working at that estate for years."

"Oh, really?" Benjamin said, stopping short. "And do you still see this friend?"

"I haven't seen him for a while, but we worked together more than twenty years ago. An amazing mechanic, believe me."

19

Behind the wheel of his Mercedes, Benjamin followed the police cruisers up the drive to the château. Ordinarily, Inspector Barbaroux would have balked at letting the winemaker accompany him on an arrest. But Benjamin insisted—almost politely. After all, his daughter had nearly been killed, and he had helped out on this investigation. Barbaroux had even admitted that his hint about giving the château a more careful reading broke the case: they found out who was next on Rinetti's firing spree. Still, Benjamin had to add to his arguments a promise to share a few bottles from his own cellar with the inspector.

"Okay, okay. I suppose it's only right that you witness the arrest," Barbaroux had finally conceded over the phone. "It's personal, right? Just remember, Mr. Cooker, keep your distance, and no funny business!"

"You have my word, Inspector," Benjamin answered.

He parked the convertible by the rosebushes and watched as Barbaroux led Stéphane Sarrazin out of the wine cellar in handcuffs. Sarrazin looked up just before the inspector pushed him into the backseat of the cruiser. Meeting Benjamin's eyes, he smirked. For a few seconds, Benjamin was glad he wasn't alone with the man. He didn't want to think of what he was capable of doing.

"I figure he'll get at least fifteen years behind bars," Barbaroux had said during their phone conversation. "And he might just spend the rest of his life there."

"I have no problem with that, Inspector."

Benjamin had been suspicious of the cellar master from the start. There was something disturbing, or rather disturbed, in Sarrazin's eyes. Too much cynicism and egotism. The cellar master was smart, but he had made a fatal mistake when he gave Virgile the case of wine.

"He never imagined his own bottles would betray him," Benjamin told the inspector. "When Stofa recognized the label, that was it. Dumb luck, but case closed."

Stofa and Sarrazin had worked together twenty-three years earlier in a garage on the Allées de Brienne. Sarrazin was talented, and everyone was surprised when he quit. Most of all Stofa. As it turned out, Sarrazin had been taking night classes to become an oenologist.

"He wasn't about to spend the rest of his life with grease under his nails," Barbaroux said. "He studied, worked hard, and took a bottom-rung job in a vineyard. After a few years with his nose to the grindstone, he landed the job of cellar master. You gotta give the guy credit for that."

"Too bad for him, he was about to lose his job too. That was the straw. The firings, the way the Moroccans were treated, Georges Moncaillou's suicide, and he was going to get shoved out the door like everyone else. He couldn't take it."

"Yes, it was as simple as that," Benjamin said. "And when he finally made the decision to get rid of Rinetti, his skills as a mechanic came in handy."

"For a while there he fooled your assistant," Barbaroux said. "Sarrazin didn't seem to have any mechanical know-how when they tried to repair the Peugeot."

"Indeed. He was a shrewd man. At our first meeting, he convinced us that he was one of the lucky few who hadn't been fired, and then when Virgile showed up, he wouldn't have dreamed of fixing the car. He didn't want to do anything that would jeopardize his cover. The French writer Paul Léautaud wrote something fitting on this very subject: 'It seems to me that being intelligent is, above all, being mistrustful, even of oneself.'"

"Is that so, Mr. Cooker? In my line of work you're always suspicious. But I make one exception: I trust my gut. Instincts, Mr. Cooker."

Benjamin watched as the cruiser with Sarrazin in the back pulled away, followed by another cruiser. Barbaroux walked over to him.

"Thank you for keeping your word. By the way, we got to the bottom of that note. It wasn't Sarrazin. It was Moncaillou's son. Like everyone else, he didn't like what was going on at the château, and he wanted to alert someone who might have some clout. It ended up being you. He had seen you on the property, and he knew who you were."

"Ah, so the last piece of the puzzle falls into place."

"Yes, so now I've got to get back to the station." Barbaroux pulled a wadded handkerchief out of his pocket and wiped his forehead. "Hope this heat wave breaks soon." He stuffed the handkerchief back in his pocket and extended his hand to the winemaker. "See you around, Mr. Cooker." He walked back to his unmarked car and drove off.

Left alone, Virgile gave the château a long look. It was perfectly quiet. No one seemed to be there. And he decided to do what he hadn't been allowed to do before. He walked toward the building and pushed open the heavy door leading to the Gayraud-Valrose wine cellar. Inside he found a scene that looked like many others. Dim lights. Crates of bottles lined up along the walls. Barrels stacked almost to the ceiling.

"An ordinary wine cellar," he said to himself. "Very ordinary."

But he thought again. Could any wine cellar be ordinary? After all, this was the place where celestials hovered above, biding their time. This was the place where miracles sometimes happened, and transformation was an everyday occurrence.

The winemaker looked up, where the angels were waiting to take their share.

"Please give your compatriots—the ones who were watching over my daughter that night—a message for me. Tell them I'm forever in their debt."

20

Margaux rose from her armchair, refusing her father's help. Leaning on her crutches, she stared into his eyes.

"Take me there!"

They settled into the convertible and took the road all the way to the tip of the Médoc. Margaux quickly glanced at the side-view mirror, where the reassuring image of Grangebelle was disappearing. Benjamin was silent. She would leave for New York in a few days, and he probably wouldn't see her again until the following summer, unless she decided to come for Christmas or there was an unexpected business trip. The telephone would be the only way they would talk. Once a week, according to the ritual from which they never deviated but which was becoming increasingly difficult to bear. The distance was beginning to weigh on him. Even if he acquiesced to her wishes and started using Skype, it wasn't enough.

They climbed aboard the ferry at Verdon-sur-Mer and followed the silty waters of the Gironde, finally reaching the stormy waves of the ocean. The heat wave had finally broken. Margaux held out her face to the sea spray, eyes closed. Benjamin knew she was waiting for the fleeting and intense moment when she would open her eyes again and see it: the silhouette emerging from the waves, colossal and stately. The Cordouan lighthouse, a surreal stone apparition, was always her reward, the promise always kept. Not a year would go by that Benjamin did not make this pilgrimage with his daughter. They would not miss this outing, which was theirs alone, for anything in the world.

The ferry left them on the sandbar, which, at low tide, allowed one to walk the rest of the way to this Versailles of the seas, a column of light erected to the glory of a king and all the sea gods. Some considered this the most beautiful light-house in the world.

Benjamin was desperate to help Margaux as she slowly navigated the ground with her crutch-es, but she waved him off with a flick of her hand. Cordouan had to be earned. Finally, at the foot of the circular base, she caught her breath and then climbed the first steps that took them to the elaborate main entrance, flanked by columns and topped with a triangular pediment. Benjamin could see Margaux casting a worried look toward the staircase leading to the other floors. Then, with a determined look, she embarked on the ascent. Benjamin trudged behind, ready to catch her if she fell backward. Margaux made few stops, reserving the pleasure of visiting the staterooms on the way back down. The climb was long, tiresome, slow, and painful for his daughter, but when they reached the top, Benjamin could see the thrill on her face as she gazed at the rumbling ocean, both threatening and mysterious.

"I'll never get tired of this, Papa. I hate the thought of leaving the world one day and never seeing this wonder again."

"I don't like it when you talk that way," Benjamin mumbled. "We must live each moment as if we were eternal."

"I was afraid we wouldn't be able to come here this year. It's probably what I would have missed the most."

"A summer without Cordouan? I can't even imagine it," Benjamin said. "And yet it almost didn't happen. You gave us quite a scare."

"But don't forget I'm a little bit American now. And over there, everything has a happy ending."

"Once your leg has healed completely, our little family can have that happy ending. We were supposed to have a quiet, uneventful visit, but we were pushed into a drama that others had written without knowing that we would be key characters. There's never any telling where God's will leads us."

"That's an interesting way to look at it, Papa."

"I sincerely believe that the author, Mr. Sarrazin, didn't count on having us in his play, and he was the first to be surprised. Now he has all the time in the world to think about it."

Margaux snuggled against her father for warmth.

"Where do you get this obsession to snoop around and find answers?" she whispered.

"I don't know. It's not so much an obsession. I'm just curious by nature."

"Have you always been like that?"

"I think so, yes. In fact, it's because of you that I developed this trait."

"Because of me? How's that?"

"Thanks to you, rather. One day, when you were about five or six, you asked me a question. I couldn't give you an answer, and I couldn't bear the look of disappointment on your face."

"Do you remember what that question was?"

"You asked me how pebbles got into your shoes when you had no holes in them."

Margaux smiled. "I don't have any memory of that. I can understand how you'd have a hard time explaining such a thing. And do you have the answer now?"

"Frankly, I don't have a one-size-fits-all answer. A pebble can make its way into a shoe in any number of ways. To get a definitive answer, you have to replicate what happened before the pebble invaded the shoe; the way you put the shoe on, whether the lace was tied correctly, the kind of terrain you were walking on, whether the leather was soft and yawned a bit, whether the shoe was the right size, whether you were just walking, or running and walking, or jumping and walking... There's a whole range of factors."

They made their way back down with heavy steps. It wrenched Benjamin's heart each time they left the lighthouse and the majestic panorama of the rolling sea. It meant that his daughter's visit would soon end. They stopped at the chapel whose twin windows let a golden light filter in. Columns crowned with Corinthian capitals reached up to the entablature. They bowed before Notre-Dame de Cordouan, and Margaux lit a candle. Benjamin watched as she gazed at the lavish bays and the royal coats of arms framed by clusters of grapes.

"Do you know if people get married in the lighthouse chapel?"

"I don't think so. I've only heard of two or three celebrations, but just for the lighthouse keepers."

"Too bad," said Margaux, a wistful look on her face.

Benjamin felt his muscles stiffen. Please, he prayed, don't let it happen until she's found the one who deserves her.

"Why? Do you have plans along those lines?"

"Who knows? I will have to think about it someday."

"You still have lots of time."

"I don't think I'll get married in the United States. I know I've talked about staying there, but I'd rather make my life with someone who shares my culture, my beliefs, and my way of life."

"Someone from Bordeaux?"

"Why not?"

"Or perhaps someone from Bergerac?" Benjamin teased without expecting a response. "Friendship between a man and a woman 'is either virgin love or new love.' I've always liked that quote."

"Would you stop with your quotations? It's annoying. Who said that anyway? I don't know how you remember all those things or how you manage to conjure them up at any given time or place."

"You should go back and read Jules Barbey d'Aurevilly instead of that gloomy crime fiction of yours."

"I'll read what I want, when I want, and where I want."

Benjamin smiled thinking how true to her namesake she was, and like a wine, he must allow her to be herself. They continued walking down the stairs, making sure his daughter had each step. At the foot of the lighthouse, he wrapped his raincoat around Margaux to protect her against the west wind. He held onto her as they walked the length of the sandbar to the ferry that would take them back to land.

"That was brave of you to climb to the top and back down on your crutches. I confess that I wondered if you would make it, but I should have known better. Once you've made your mind up, there's no changing it."

"That's true. I counted the steps, if only so I could tell the story after I've ditched these crutches. There are exactly three hundred and one of them."

"I'm not sure about that," Benjamin said.

"Three hundred and one, I'm telling you. You can go check if that makes you happy."

"To be precise, there are three hundred and twenty-six. You forgot the twenty-five steps you have to climb to get to the base of the lighthouse. You counted from the big stone stairway."

"Argh! Why do you always have to have to be right?"

"Because I'm more thick-headed than you are, my child."

Margaux let her crutches drop and stood on one foot while she put her arms around her father's neck and kissed him on the cheek. Benjamin held on tight to keep her from losing her balance.

"I love you too much, you stubborn old mule. And if that makes you happy, I'm glad to let you have the last word."

Benjamin would have given up a lifetime of last words if it meant keeping her from flying off to the other side of the ocean again. But that wasn't going to happen. So he sighed and treasured this moment, when his little girl was once again tucked in his protective arms.

Thank you for reading Mayhem in Margaux.

We invite you to share your thoughts and reactions on your favorite social media and retail platforms.

We appreciate your support.

THE WINEMAKER DETECTIVE SERIES

A total epicurean immersion in French countryside and gourmet attitude with two expert
winemakers turned amateur sleuths gumshoeing
around wine country. The following titles are
currently available in English.

Treachery in Bordeaux

Barrels at the prestigious grand cru Moniales
Haut-Brion wine estate in Bordeaux have been
contaminated. Is it negligence or sabotage? Cooker
and his assistant Virgile Lanssien search the city
and the vineyards for answers, giving readers and
inside view of this famous wine region.

www.treacheryinbordeaux.com

Grand Cru Heist

After Benjamin Cooker's world gets turned upside
down one night in Paris, he retreats to the region
around Tours to recover. There, he and his assistant Virgile turn PI to solve two murders and very
particular heist. Who stole those bottles of grand
cru classé?

www.grandcruheist.com

Nightmare in Burgundy

The Winemaker Detective leaves his native Bordeaux for a dream wine tasting trip to Burgundy that turns into a troubling nightmare when he stumbles upon a mystery revolving around messages from another era. What do they mean? What dark secrets from the deep past are haunting the Clos de Vougeot?

www.nightmareinburgundy.com

Deadly Tasting

In a new Winemaker Detective adventure, a serial killer stalks Bordeaux. To understand the wine-related symbolism, the local police call on the famous wine critic Benjamin Cooker. The investigation leads them to the dark hours of France's history, as the mystery thickens among the once-peaceful vineyards of Pomerol.

www.deadlytasting.com

Cognac Conspiracies

The heirs to one of the oldest Cognac estates in France face a hostile takeover by foreign investors. Renowned wine expert Benjamin Cooker is called in to audit the books. In what he thought was a sleepy provincial town, he and his assistant Virgile have their loyalties tested.

www.cognacconspiracies.com

ABOUT THE AUTHORS

Noël Balen (left) and Jean-Pierre Alaux (right).
(©David Nakache)

Jean-Pierre Alaux and **Noël Balen** came up with the Winemaker Detective over a glass of wine, of course. Jean-Pierre Alaux is a magazine, radio, and television journalist when he is not writing novels in southwestern France. He is a genuine wine and food lover, and won the Antonin Carême prize for his cookbook *La Truffe sur le Soufflé*, which he wrote with the chef Alexis Pélissou. He is the grandson of a winemaker and exhibits a real passion for wine and winemaking. For him, there is no greater common denominator than wine. Coauthor of the series Noël Balen lives in Paris, where he shares his time between writing, making records, and lecturing on music. He plays bass, is a music critic, and has authored a number of books about musicians, in addition to his novel and short-story writing.

About the Translator

Sally Pane studied French at State University of New York Oswego and the Sorbonne before receiving her master's degree in French literature from the University of Colorado, where she wrote *Camus and the Americas: A Thematic Analysis of Three Works Based on His Journaux de Voyage.* Her career includes more than twenty years of translating and teaching French and Italian at Berlitz and at University of Colorado Boulder. She has translated a number of titles in the Winemaker Detective series. In addition to her passion for French, she has studied Italian. She lives in Boulder, Colorado, with her husband.

DISCOVER MORE BOOKS FROM

LE FRENCH BOOK
www.lefrenchbook.com

Shadow Ritual
www.shadowritual.com

The Paris Homicide series by Frédérique Molay
www.parishomicide.com

The Paris Lawyer **by Sylvie Granotier**
www.theparislawyer.com

The Greenland Breach **by Bernard Besson**
www.thegreenlandbreach.com

Consortium thrillers by David Khara
www.theconsortiumthrillers.com